"I'm not lying," he said with exaggerated calm.

"Oh, please." Candy's eyes danced, as if she enjoyed tormenting him. Maybe she did. Maybe he enjoyed it, too...just the smallest possible amount. "As Buddy the Elf once said to the department store Santa, 'You sit on a throne of lies.'"

Dan almost smiled, and just as he caught himself, a sizzling noise pierced the strange tension between them. The lights in the interior of the duplex behind Candy flickered before going completely dark. The fan powering Godzilla the reindeer sputtered and then stopped. Dan ducked for cover as the giant animal swayed and then began to slowly deflate, but not before a puffy antler sent him colliding into Candy.

His hands closed into fists around her impossibly soft sweater. She smelled like sugarplums and royal icing—like Christmas itself.

Dan's breath clogged in his throat.

When she spoke, her voice hummed through him with enough electricity to power an entire herd of inflatable caribou. "Son of a nutcracker."

Dear Reader,

Welcome back to Lovestruck! *Merry Christmas, Baby* is the fourth and final book in my Lovestruck, Vermont series for Harlequin Special Edition. I've so enjoyed working on this series! The Lovestruck series is a group of four interconnected books about newcomers to a charming small town where love comes in packages.

Candy Cane is a heroine who lives up to her name. As a producer for made-for-television Christmas movies, she *lives* Christmas, twenty-four hours a day, 365 days a year. But when she unexpectedly becomes the guardian for her infant cousin, her holiday world is turned upside down. It's as if she's in a snow globe to which someone has given a good hard shake. After being temporarily fired, Candy is determined to give baby Faith the perfect Christmas holiday—which should be easy peasy. Christmas is Candy's specialty...or so she thinks.

Dr. Dan Manning, Lovestruck's beloved small-town pediatrician, is doing his best to get through the holiday season, just like he does every December. The last thing he needs is a new neighbor who's literally named after a peppermint stick. She loves Christmas as much as he loathes the holiday, but when a Christmas Eve snowstorm blows into town, these two opposites find out they just might have more in common than they realize.

I love Christmas stories. The holidays are a hopeful, glorious time of year. I hope this Christmas finds you happy, healthy and brimming with hope. Thank you for letting me be a part of it through these words.

Merry Christmas and happy reading!

Teri

Merry Christmas, Baby

TERI WILSON

HARLEQUIN

SPECIAL
EDITION

Recycling programs for this product may not exist in your area.

ISBN-13: 978-1-335-40823-5

Merry Christmas, Baby

Copyright © 2021 by Teri Wilson

Harlequin Enterprises ULC
22 Adelaide St. West, 40th Floor
Toronto, Ontario M5H 4E3, Canada
www.Harlequin.com

Printed in U.S.A.

Teri Wilson is a *Publishers Weekly* bestselling author of romance and romantic comedy. Several of Teri's books have been adapted into Hallmark Channel Original Movies, most notably *Unleashing Mr. Darcy*. She is also a recipient of the prestigious RITA® Award for excellence in romance fiction for her novel *The Bachelor's Baby Surprise*. Teri has a major weakness for cute animals and pretty dresses, and she loves following the British royal family. Visit her at www.teriwilson.net.

Books by Teri Wilson

Harlequin Special Edition

Lovestruck, Vermont

Baby Lessons
Firehouse Christmas Baby
The Trouble with Picket Fences

Furever Yours

How to Rescue a Family

Wilde Hearts

The Ballerina's Secret
How to Romance a Runaway Bride
The Bachelor's Baby Surprise
A Daddy by Christmas

Montana Mavericks: Six Brides for Six Brothers

The Maverick's Secret Baby

HQN

Unmasking Juliet
Unleashing Mr. Darcy

Visit the Author Profile page
at Harlequin.com for more titles.

In loving memory
of my husband's dear friend, Dan Decker.
We miss you, Dan. xoxo

Chapter One

Oh, here it comes.

Candy's eyes grew misty and her heart gave a little squeeze as the couple directly in her line of vision gazed at one another though a lacy veil of snow flurries.

The perfect Christmas kiss.

It didn't matter how many times Candy had witnessed such moments—and she'd witnessed *plenty* of them, so many that she'd lost count—she got weepy every single time. Her boss, Gabe, liked to call her a hopeless romantic. Maybe he was right. Or maybe she was too softhearted for her own good. Either way, nothing made her swoon quite like a winter wonderland Christmas kiss.

Candy felt herself smile from the inside out. Visions of mistletoe danced in her head as the man lowered his gaze and the woman rose up on tiptoe, their lips just a whisper apart. Christmas lights glittered behind the happy couple, bathing them in the warm glow of holiday magic.

It was all so lovely. So tender. So perfect. Candy heard someone let out a dreamy sigh, and then realized it was her. The man cupped the woman's face in his hands, and their breath mingled together in a delicate, frosty puff of air. Candy didn't dare move. Even the snow flurries seemed to be holding their breath in anticipation.

And then, just as the woman's mittened hands balled into giddy fists and the man's lips brushed against hers, the wail of a baby pierced the tremulous silence...

Everything—the kiss, the magic, even the snowflakes—came to an abrupt halt. Someone beside Candy let out a groan. The man and woman both turned toward her and glared.

"Cut!" Gabe bellowed.

Candy jumped at the sound of his voice. At sixty-four, Gabe had directed more than fifty made-for-television movies over the course of his career, but he wasn't normally a bellower. Then again, Candy—Gabe's favorite assistant director—didn't usually turn up for work with an infant strapped to her chest in a BabyBjörn.

"Sorry." Candy winced and began doing the bouncy little dance that baby Faith seemed to love. "That was totally my fault."

"Yes, I'm aware." Gabe cast a pointed glance at the back of Faith's downy head.

Candy rested a protective hand on the baby's tiny back and bounced with renewed vigor. "I got caught up in the moment and stopped bouncing. It won't happen again."

"Candy." Gabe pinched the bridge of his nose the way he always did when something on set went horribly wrong. Candy had seen him do it dozens, if not hundreds, of times before. She just wasn't accustomed to being the troublesome *something* in question. "This isn't working."

Candy nodded. "I know, but the nanny that the service sent over this morning was terrible. She had a definite serial killer vibe. I couldn't leave Faith with her."

"That's what you said about the nanny they sent over yesterday." Gabe sighed. "And the day before that."

Candy's face went warm. "Right, but…"

"Maybe you've worked on one too many stalker movies," Brian, the second assistant director, said with a smirk.

Impossible. Candy didn't work on stalker films. She was all about Christmas movies, 365 days a year. Candy *adored* Christmas. She always had.

It was her parents' fault, really. Honestly, no one had any business naming a child Candy Cane, other than Santa Claus himself.

Santa wasn't real, though. Candy knew this. She might be a little Christmas-obsessed, but she wasn't delusional. The baby currently kicking her little feet in glee, oblivious to her recent film set faux pas, however, *was* real. And she'd managed to turn Candy's life completely upside down in less than a week.

"Let's take five," Gabe said, bellowing yet again.

Then he cast a meaningful look at Brian. Brian removed his headset, placed it gently on top of one of the video monitors in "video village," the area on set where the production team always gathered, and quietly walked away.

Weird. Brian's mannerisms were usually more of the bull-in-a-china-shop variety. But it was getting late. The shoot was already running over an hour behind. He was probably just tired.

Candy took a deep breath. *One more scene and then we wrap.*

She nodded to herself as the stand-ins took the places of the lead actress and actor and the stars headed toward their respective trailers. She could do this, baby and all. Once they nailed the Christmas kiss, she'd have an entire week before postproduction started.

A week was enough time to adjust to the fact that she had a baby now, wasn't it?

Faith squirmed in her BabyBjörn, and Candy's heart squeezed tight. The poor little thing was just as lost as Candy was, wasn't she?

Candy pressed a tender kiss to the top of the baby's head. *We're in this together, kid. Just you and me.* They'd figure things out. They had to. Candy didn't have much of a choice in the matter.

That's not technically true, though, is it? a voice in the back of Candy's head whispered. Her stomach squirmed and she pushed it away.

"Candy, we need to talk," Gabe said. He wasn't bellowing anymore. In fact, his tone had gone quiet. *Too* quiet, if the way the rest of the production scattered like mice was any indication.

"Okay." Candy nodded, continuing to bounce as Faith gurgled in delight.

"A film set is no place for a baby," Gabe said.

Again, Candy knew this. They hardly even used live infants onscreen, opting for dolls instead. Once, a doll's foot had fallen off and no one noticed until the movie aired on Christmas Eve. But Candy figured now wasn't the time to remind Gabe of that embarrassing mistake.

"I know." Candy swallowed. "Look, you know I'm just as surprised by this as you are."

Before last week, Candy hadn't even been aware of her second cousin on her father's side and now here she was, raising said cousin's baby.

"My condolences to your family," Gabe said. He couldn't seem to look Candy in the eyes anymore. "But…"

"But what? You're not about to fire me, are you?" Candy laughed.

Gabe was as much a father figure as he was an actual boss. They celebrated Thanksgiving together and most other major holidays, too, since they were typically shooting on location ten months out of the year. Gabe loved dad jokes, and he wore fanny packs nonironically. He made movies about finding the true meaning of Christmas, with montages of snowball fights and gingerbread house decorating.

Gabe would *never* fire Candy. Ever.

"Yes, I'm firing you," he said.

Candy shook her head. "No."

Gabe nodded. "Yes."

Faith kicked her little legs again, and this time, one of her dainty baby feet made contact with Gabe's fanny pack.

Candy took a small backward step and lowered her voice in case anyone on set could overhear the most humiliating conversation of her entire career. "Gabe, please. This doesn't even make sense. We're wrapping tonight."

He arched one of his furry, overgrown eyebrows. "We should have wrapped hours ago."

"I know, but..."

"But like I said, this just isn't working." He waved a hand toward Exhibit A, Faith. Then his features softened, but not his resolve. "I've asked Brian to step in as first AD for postproduction."

Ouch. Candy's pride took a serious hit. She'd *trained* Brian, for goodness' sake.

"Okay. Right. Well, that's not ideal, but maybe you're right." Candy nodded, as if trying to talk herself into accepting this humbling news with a modicum of dignity.

There was no need to panic. So she'd miss a week of editing, sound mixing and color correction. She could live with that, even though the thought of Brian putting together the opening and closing credits instead of her was enough to make her sick to her stomach. The man had horrendous taste in fonts.

Truthfully, Candy could use an extra week to get her new life as a parent in order. In fourteen days' time, she needed to be in northern Ontario to shoot another Christmas film. Which meant she needed to find child care arrangements in a foreign country. It also meant she needed to get a passport for Faith.

Did infants even need passports?

Ugh, she knew nothing about babies. Until six days ago, she'd never even changed a diaper. But she'd figured it out, hadn't she? She could figure out how to be a stellar assistant director and a mom at the same time, too.

"I'm glad you understand. You're doing a

good thing, Candy. A noble thing. And I support you wholeheartedly, you know that. A few months off will do wonders," Gabe said.

"Months?" Candy froze. She didn't have a springy little bounce left in her. Faith immediately started fussing. "What are you talking about? We've got another picture on deck in just two weeks, remember? We're shooting a Christmas movie during the actual Christmas holidays, for a change. In northern Canada, with *real* snow."

Candy had worked her butt off securing that location. It was perfect. There was only one place in the entire Northern Hemisphere that would have been better.

"I'm taking you off the next one, too." Gabe gave her a gentle smile—so gentle that Candy wanted to cry. Or maybe the tears pricking her eyes were simply the natural result of watching her career go up in smoke.

This was the twenty-first century. Weren't women supposed to be able to have it all? That's what all the magazines said. Although, truth be told, Candy had never wanted to have it all. She wasn't greedy. She hadn't planned this. She would have been completely satisfied with an Emmy Award instead of a baby. But now that she had the latter, it didn't seem fair that she should have to forgo the former.

"It's just a break, kid, not forever," Gabe said as Faith's fussing turned into full-on cries. "Maybe not for months, but at least until after the holidays."

Candy started bouncing again, but this time she wasn't sure if she was simply trying to comfort the baby or the both of them. "What am I supposed to do in the meantime? Where am I supposed to go…?"

The final two words lodged in her throat. She couldn't seem to make herself say them.

For Christmas. Where was she supposed to go for Christmas?

Gabe knew good and well that Candy's parents had passed away years ago. Once upon a time, she'd had a perfect Christmas kiss—a real one, with real snow and real mistletoe and real fairy lights that had fallen around her like stardust. Just days later, her entire world had fallen apart, and no other Christmas had been the same. Not even the perfect, pretend holidays she'd spent a lifetime creating.

"Candy, I love you like a daughter. Don't you think it's time you had a real holiday instead of this?" Gabe waved his big arms, encompassing the enormous cameras, the maze of electrical cables and a plethora of holiday props. Cardboard gingerbread houses decorated with glue to look like frosting. Flocked, artificial evergreen trees dotted with crystals and plastic pine cones. Acrylic icicles dripping from the park bench where the stand-ins stood waiting for the real stars to come back to their marks. "Don't you think you owe that to Faith?"

Faith.

Candy's throat squeezed closed. As usual, Gabe was right. She had a daughter now—a tiny baby who'd just experienced the worst possible twist of fate that life had to offer a small child. It was too late for Candy to go back and fix her own imperfect life, but she could still give Faith the one thing that had slipped through Candy's fingers years ago.

A *real* family Christmas.

She lifted her chin and met Gabe's gaze. "You promise you'll take me back after the New Year?"

Gabe tilted his head. "If that's still what you want, then yes. I promise. Now take that baby and get out of here."

"Trust me, it's what I want. Don't you dare offer the job to Brian without talking to me first." She couldn't believe she even had to say those words, but after being fired on the last day of shooting, Candy wasn't sure what to think about anything anymore—save for one thing.

If she wanted to give Faith a real Christmas, she knew exactly where to go.

Dr. Dan Manning shrugged out of his white coat and smoothed down his novelty tie. This one was a brown silk with a red fuzzball nose, googly eyes and comically huge antlers protruding from either side, mere inches below his Windsor knot. A necktie homage to Santa's most famous reindeer.

As the sole pediatrician in Lovestruck, Vermont, Dan was rather famous for his novelty ties. They were great icebreakers with the kids, especially the ones who came to his office with an injury or sick with the flu. It was amazing what a pair of plastic eyeballs and a strip of fabric could do. Since he'd opened his practice five years ago, Dan's tie collection had grown by leaps and bounds. The master closet in his duplex in Lovestruck's quaint historic district was practically overflowing with them.

As much as Dan appreciated a comical tie, he wasn't such a fan of the Rudolph monstrosity currently dangling from his neck. In all honesty, he loathed it. But Rudolph had been a Christmas gift last year from his nurse, Frances. And Frances, like everyone else in Lovestruck, expected him to be all decked out in Christmas cheer this time of year. Not wearing it would have been a crime, so Dan did his best to ignore his inner Grinch voice and wore the blasted thing.

He loosened his Windsor knot ever so slightly.

"Not so fast," Frances said as she breezed into his office on her Christmas crocs. They were a garish green with white fur trim and looked like something Buddy the Elf would wear. Because of course they did. "You might want to put that coat back on. We have a last-minute walk-in."

"An emergency?" Dan reached for his coat.

Frances didn't seem ultra-alarmed, so it must not be too serious. Then again, it took a lot to ruffle Frances's feathers.

"You could say that. Diane Foster's two-year-old stuck a popcorn kernel up his nose." Frances's gaze darted briefly to the red Rudolph nose on Dan's tie and she looked away.

Dan sighed. "Let me guess—the popcorn kernel is somehow Christmas-related."

"They were stringing popcorn garland for their Christmas tree. It's not a crime, you know." Frances jammed a hand on her hip. "Honestly, sometimes I worry about you. You can be downright Scroogey."

Guilty as charged. "It's just a little much, don't you think? This place is like Hallmark on steroids in December. Last night I saw a live camel walking down Main Street."

Frances shrugged one shoulder. "Of course you did. The living nativity scene started last night."

"A *live camel*, Frances." That just wasn't normal. Or safe. It was below freezing outside. Camels were desert animals. Could they handle that sort of extreme weather?

Never mind. Dan was a pediatrician, not a veterinarian. Although, this was Lovestruck. About six months ago, the fire chief had asked him if it was possible to prescribe Valium to a cat named Fancy who was apparently terrorizing the entire LFD. Anything was possible around here.

"Fine. If you're so kamilaphobic, stay home tonight and skip the living nativity play, but you've still got Diane Foster's toddler to worry about." Frances shoved a nasal aspirator at him, which, miraculously, hadn't been adorned with antlers or a tiny felt Santa hat.

Dan arched a brow. "Kamilaphobic?"

"Fear of camels." Frances shot him a smug grin. "It was one of the words in the crossword puzzle in the *Bee* a few days ago."

"Nice." Dan nodded. "But for the record, I'm not afraid of camels."

"Oh, that's right. It's just Christmas cheer that scares you. I stand corrected." Frances shifted her weight from one hideous elf croc to the other.

"Not afraid of that, either," he said, heading toward the door, nasal aspirator in hand. A popcorn kernel-ectomy was beginning to seem much more pleasant than this conversation.

"Whatever you say," Frances said, falling in line behind him. "You know, if you'd actually get out and about this time of year, you'd see it's really not so bad. You might even like it."

Not a chance. "Frances, remember when we talked about personal boundaries during your performance review last month?"

Dan hated to pull the boss card. He really did—but not as much as he hated December in his chocolate box of a hometown.

"Point taken," Frances muttered. "But one more thing, boss?"

Dan paused at the closed door to the exam room where his tiny patient was waiting for him to remedy the unfortunate garland situation. "Dare I ask?"

"Your new tenant stopped by earlier to pick up her key." Frances's face lit up like a (Dan hated to admit) Christmas tree. "Did you know she came all the way from California?"

Dan was, in fact, privy to this information. Lovestruck was as quaint and wholesome as a small town could be, but he wasn't an idiot. He knew better than to give the key to the other half of the duplex to just anyone.

"As a matter of fact, I do," Dan said.

Ms. Candace Cane was a resident of Los Angeles, with one child, and she'd paid her entire month's rent up front, along with the customary security deposit.

Wait a minute. He felt himself frown. His tenant's name was Candace Cane…as in Candy Cane? How on earth had he let that slip past him?

"She's a new mom." Frances shrugged. "Well, sort of. She just became the guardian for her orphaned cousin. Isn't that just the saddest thing you've ever heard? Anyhoo, she must be a special person."

Dan had known about the baby, but not the specifics. But Frances knew, because of course she did.

"She's in show business." Frances's eyes danced. "She makes those Christmas movies for television that everyone loves so much."

His gut churned. She could *not* be serious.

"Not everyone," he countered. The Rudolph tie felt stifling all of a sudden, like he was being strangled by Santa's entire stable of reindeer. "And how do you know so much personal information about my tenant, anyway?"

"Boundaries. Right." Frances pulled a face. "Sorry, boss. Go ahead and give me the talk again."

Dan sighed. Why bother? Frances was a busybody and that wasn't going to change. Luckily, she was also a fantastic nurse—the best Dan had ever seen.

Besides, he had bigger problems to deal with at the moment than Frances's boundary issues. Perhaps even bigger than a popcorn kernel lodged where it wasn't supposed to be.

This time of year was always a struggle for Dan. He just wanted to keep his head down and get through the holiday season, and now he apparently would have to do that while sharing the duplex with a woman who'd just walked straight off the set of a Christmas movie and was named after a peppermint stick.

His head throbbed as he reached for the doorknob to the exam room. One of the googly eyes on his tie rolled back and forth, as if it were trying to wink at him.

Joy to the world.

Chapter Two

There was a reason that Christmas movies never showed people flying clear across the country during the holidays with babies in tow. Candy just hadn't been aware of said reason until she was forced to escort an infant all the way from California to Vermont herself.

In *coach*, thank you very much.

Whenever Gabe or a nameless, faceless production company was footing the bill, Candy got to fly in business class, where the champagne was free and her seat reclined completely flat, like an actual bed. Babies were also conspicuously absent in business class, although their absence had never really registered with Candy before. Probably because, until a few weeks ago, she'd been blissfully baby-free.

At least she'd thought she'd been blissful. If that had been true, it seemed like she would've been able to decline Faith's guardianship. Despite the fact that becoming a mom (of sorts) completely out of the blue had turned her entire life upside down, she never even considered turning Faith over to social services.

No.

Way.

Even if it meant that *Brian* was now doing the postproduction work on *her* movie. Ugh, Candy couldn't even think about that. Besides, she was in Lovestruck now. She had spit-up down the front of her adorably ugly Christmas sweater and Cheerios in her hair, but—*hallelujah*—she was in Vermont. She could practically hear a choir singing Handel in her imagination right now.

Fun fact: Handel's *Messiah* was old enough to be in the public domain, so it was totally free to use for movie purposes. But being a really powerful piece of music, it had a tendency to upstage anything onscreen, so Gabe routinely shot Candy down whenever she suggested they use it.

Gabe wasn't here right now, though. And for once in her life, Candy was living in the real world, not a movie set, so she hummed the Hallelujah Chorus to herself as she left her rental duplex and pushed Faith's brand-new high-tech stroller toward Lovestruck's charming town square. Sidenote—the stroller wasn't nearly as simple to fold into an overhead-bin-sized square as the instructions implied. Candy had been reduced to tears trying to get that thing shoved out of sight in time for takeoff. Luckily, a kind flight attendant had come to her rescue.

The flight was behind her now, though. An hour ago, Candy had picked up her key from Dr. Dan Manning's office on Main Street, just a block away from the historic district where his gorgeous Tiffany-blue-colored Victorian duplex stood on the corner in all of its white picket fence and gingerbread-trimmed glory. The house was stunning—even prettier than it had looked online—with one notable exception. It was the only home on the block that was completely unadorned for the holidays. No wreath on the door, no swags of evergreen hanging jauntily from the crisp white fence, not a single illuminated Christmas bulb twinkling from the eaves.

Clearly the good doctor, whom Candy had yet to meet, had been too busy to get around to decorating. He'd probably been distracted by saving young lives, or maybe he'd worn himself out decking the halls of his pediatric office, because whoa, it straight up looked like the North Pole in there. The nurse who'd given Candy the key had been wearing a pair of hilariously gaudy Christmas crocs. Candy could hardly wait to meet Dr. Manning himself. He probably had a white Santa beard and a belly that shook like a bowlful of jelly. Candy would've bet money on it.

Adorable. She inhaled a deep breath of frosty air as she pushed Faith's stroller along the sidewalk. *Everything about this town is adorable.*

Somewhere over the Midwest, as Candy had munched on airplane peanuts and prayed for Faith to fall asleep, she'd started to wonder if this entire trip had been a truly terrible idea. After all, Candy had been twelve years old the last time she'd set foot anywhere near Lovestruck. Could it really be as perfect as she'd remembered it?

Yes. Yes, it could. The old-fashioned lampposts along Main Street were wrapped in red and white ribbons to look like candy canes, swags of evergreen and twinkle lights stretched overhead from one side of the street to the other, and a huge blue spruce stood in front of the coffee shop at Lovestruck's biggest intersection, towering over sweet little mom-and-pop businesses and one-of-a-kind boutiques. Best of all, everything was blanketed with a fine, pristine layer of sparkling snow—*real* snow, not the foamy stuff that Candy usually had to have sprayed every half hour with a big, noisy machine that took multiple people and a staggering amount of electricity to operate.

Honestly, Candy couldn't have designed a more perfect holiday tableau if she'd been handed a million-dollar budget and the industry's hardest-working crew. The travel stress had totally been worth it. She and baby Faith were about to have a picture-perfect Christmas. How could they not, in a place like this?

She aimed the stroller in the direction of the coffee shop—named the Bean, how cute was that?—and grinned as she blinked against the crisp winter breeze. Her eyes were watering like crazy. Thirty degrees was quite cold, wasn't it? She might need to invest in a new coat. Her ruffled Burberry trench was *not* cutting it, and Faith definitely needed one of those baby snowsuits that sort of looked like astronaut outfits. But first, caffeine.

Minutes later, she wedged Faith's stroller next to a booth at the Bean and warmed her hands on a peppermint mocha. Just as she was about to take her first sip, a woman with red hair slid into the booth opposite her and stuck out her hand.

"Hi, welcome to Lovestruck. I'm Diane Foster." She smiled brightly as she pumped Candy's hand up and down. Then she waved her perfectly manicured fingertips toward the toddler sleeping in the stroller she'd parked beside Faith's. "And this is my son, Joey."

"Nice to meet you." Candy glanced at Joey. "He's very...cute."

Candy was being polite. Joey very probably was cute. It was just kind of hard to tell when the child was conked out with his head lolling to one side and had a large Band-Aid decorated with the snowman from *Frozen* plastered across his nose.

"Don't pay any attention to the bandage. We had a little accident with popcorn garland earlier." Diane's smile grew a bit strained around the edges. "Anyway, I just wanted to make sure you had a chance to meet Joey. Also, just so you know, he's had experience in child pageants and is extremely photogenic."

She reached into her purse, pulled out a Christmas card emblazoned with a family holiday portrait and slapped it down on the table in front of Candy. Sure enough, there was little Joey, looking up at her from the picture, wearing a Santa hat and a completely unnatural-looking smile on his face.

"Lovely," Candy said.

She took a gulp of her latte. She wasn't accustomed to making mom-friends. Was this how it was done? Was she supposed to start rattling items off Faith's nonexistent child résumé?

"So." Diane drummed her fingernails on the tabletop. "When does filming begin?"

"What?" Candy blinked.

Oh. *Ohhhh.* Now she knew what was going on.

"You've apparently heard that I'm involved in film." She shook her head and laughed. News really traveled fast around here, didn't it? "But I'm not here to make a movie. My daughter and I are just in Lovestruck for the holidays. We're on vacation."

So many strange new words to wrap her head around—*vacation*…my *daughter* and I.

Diane's face fell as her dreams of Joey becoming a child star went up in smoke. "Really?"

Candy nodded. "Really."

Diane took a deep breath and regrouped. "Well, we're definitely available to travel in case you need a cute child lead in your next—"

"You know what?" Candy grabbed her drink and scrambled out of the booth. "I actually need to get going. We just got here and I haven't even had a chance to unpack."

Diane started to protest, but Joey woke up, rubbed his injured nose and then scrunched his face as he began to cry.

Poor kid. Candy bit her lip, tempted to stay and make sure he was okay. But Candy knew a stage mother when she saw one, and she wasn't sure when she might have another chance for an escape.

"So nice to meet you. Merry Christmas," she called as she darted out of the Bean, inasmuch as it was possible to dart anywhere while juggling a latte, a baby stroller and accompanying baby.

Candy pushed through the door, back outside in Lovestruck's winter wonderland. Her face went numb within seconds, but she didn't care, because just beyond the grand blue spruce that stood at the entrance to the town square, she spotted the landmark she'd most been hoping to see.

Oh, my. Candy's hand flew to her throat. Memories flickered through her mind like a slow-motion film, but better and more romantic than any movie she'd ever made. Her heart gave a little squeeze. *There it is.*

The gazebo stood in the center of the town square's park area, even bigger and brighter than Candy remembered it—as perfect and white as the surrounding snow, glittering with hundreds of fairy lights. Like something out of a dream.

Candy couldn't believe it. She'd been almost afraid to look for the gazebo, in case it had been torn down sometime in the past fifteen years. But here it stood, like a monument to her favorite holiday memory—that ever-elusive, perfect Christmas kiss. The kiss had also been Candy's first, making it even more special. Perhaps that's why she'd been attempting to re-create the moment on film for her entire adult life. No matter how hard she tried, it never came close.

Because if there was one thing more dreamy

and romantic than Hollywood magic, it was *Christmas* magic.

It hit her all at once right then—the fact that she was here, in Lovestruck, with a baby of her own. She had a family again, after so many years of being alone. And Candy wanted to give Faith the kind of nostalgic childhood Christmas she deserved, the kind that Candy had experienced… once upon a time.

Dare she go sit in the gazebo? She couldn't resist. It almost felt like stepping through a looking glass.

But as soon as Candy took her first step, another beaming stage mother with a toddler in tow stepped into her path, followed quickly by an aspiring Instagram influencer who tried to shove her glossy headshots into Faith's stroller. It was official: word had gotten out that Candy was in town, and Lovestruck had suddenly gone Christmas movie crazy.

Dan didn't set out to go to the town gazebo after he left his office, but his footsteps led him there all the same. It happened sometimes. He'd learned a long time ago not to fight it, even during the holidays.

The gazebo was like a chill zone, a place

where he could just sit and shake off the stress of the day. Which is why he slowed to a stop as soon as he climbed the three steps up into the quaint wooden octagon and realized there was a woman sitting on the park bench inside.

His park bench.

There were snowflakes in her hair, and she was wearing a pair of red Fair Isle mittens decorated with elegant prancing reindeer that put his antler tie to shame.

He turned to go before she saw him, but he was a beat too late. She looked up from the baby stroller parked beside her and locked eyes with him. Dan froze, rooted to the spot by her soft brown eyes.

She heaved a mighty sigh and shook her head. "Sorry, but no."

"I beg your pardon." Dan felt himself frown.

Was she trying to forbid him from sitting down? Not that he wanted to…

He had, after all, been gunning for a quick getaway. Still, she didn't *own* the gazebo. It was a public place. He didn't need her permission to enjoy it.

Leave. Just leave now, before it gets awkward.

"I don't know what you heard, but I'm just

here on vacation. I promise I'm not looking for anyone." The woman's gaze swept over him— up, down and back again. "And no offense, but even if I did need someone, you're all wrong."

Too late, Dan thought. Awkwardness achieved. He gave her a tight smile. "No offense taken."

A lie, obviously. Dan was definitely offended. He'd just been judged based purely on his physical appearance by a woman wearing a ruffly trench coat and a gaudy holiday sweater, and he'd been found lacking.

"Don't take it the wrong the way. You're really handsome." She shrugged and her mass of loose blond curls tumbled over her shoulder. She looked like a Christmas angel—the most overembellished, garish angel Dan had ever set eyes on. "In fact, you're too handsome, if I'm being honest."

Dan narrowed his gaze at her. Why was he still standing there, exactly? Oh right, he'd been paralyzed by conversational whiplash.

"It's a thing. Truly. All of this—" she gestured at him, as if to encompass the general aura of his excess handsomeness "—would distract from the lead actor and actress. That's a big no-no. Extras are supposed to sort of blend into the background. In fact, most industry people actually call them that. *To their faces.* Can you imagine? As in, 'action, background' or 'cut, background.' I try not to do that. It just seems sort of mean."

It was like she was speaking a foreign language. Dan didn't know what to think, except that he desperately wished he'd walked straight home instead of taking the scenic route through the town square.

And then he remembered what Frances had told him earlier about his new tenant.

She's in show business. She makes those Christmas movies for television that everyone loves so much.

This must be her, the ridiculously named Candace Cane.

His temples throbbed. December was going to be a heck of a long month.

"Let me get this straight." Dan crossed his arms over his googly-eyed reindeer tie. "You think I'm angling for an audition to be an extra in a made-for-cable holiday movie?"

She blinked. "You want to be a *lead*? With no experience? That's a tad arrogant, don't you think?"

Dan barked out a laugh. *Unbelievable.* He

was the least arrogant person in this gazebo, including Candace Cane's sleeping baby.

"And just a tip, your outfit choice is a little too on the nose." She glanced at his necktie's red puffball Rudolph nose. "So to speak. On a real audition, it's better to just dress as plain and classic as possible, sort of like a blank canvas."

Says the woman who's wearing a sweater with actual Christmas tree garland hanging off it.

Dan held up a hand. "Just so we're clear, you've got this all wrong. I have zero interest in being in a Christmas movie. I don't even *like* Christmas."

Frances didn't know the half of it. Dan was as Scroogey as they came.

The woman's gaze dropped to his tie again, and her pretty bow-shaped lips curved into a smile. "Is that so?"

Dan yanked at his Windsor knot, slid the tie over his head and shoved it into the pocket of his wool overcoat.

"Better." Candace Cane nodded. The baby in the stroller started making sweet gurgling sounds, and she gently rocked it back and forth with a mittened hand. "But as I said, I'm only here on vacation. I'm totally not a filmmaker right now. I'm just a regular person and an, um, mom."

Dan studied her. He'd been in this woman's presence less than five minutes, but somehow he knew that Candace Cane was anything but regular.

He rolled his shoulders. Was it bad that he was going to enjoy setting her straight? Probably. Maybe he really was arrogant—just a smidge.

"And I'm totally not an actor right now. Or 'background.'" Dan made air quotes with his fingers, like a jerk. But this entire interaction was getting on his last nerve. "I'm just a regular person and a doctor."

The rocking motion Candace was making with the stroller stalled to a stop. He could practically see the wheels spinning in her head as she realized her mistake.

What did they call a moment like this in the movies? A meet-cute? Dan snorted. *Minus the cute part, maybe.*

Candace Cane swallowed. "A doctor?"

"Yes." He aimed a meaningful glance at the baby. Her tiny fingers were wrapped around a stuffed toy shaped like a holiday gingerbread man. Of course. "A pediatrician, actually."

"Oh," she said, and the color drained slowly from her beautiful face.

Dan arched a brow. Yeah, the conversation had definitely taken an enjoyable turn. "I'm also your new landlord."

Chapter Three

It was an honest mistake—that's what Candy kept telling herself. And yet, every time she thought about her run-in with Dr. Dan Manning at the gazebo, she felt mortified to her very core.

And now here she was, a full twenty-four hours later, still thinking about it...and still very much mortified.

Really, though, how was she supposed to have known he was her landlord, of all things? She'd just been accosted by no less than *half a dozen* Lovestruck locals who'd wanted parts in whatever movie they thought she'd come to town to film. Someone should probably change the name of this town to Starstruck.

Candy still couldn't figure out how word had spread. She didn't know a soul in Lovestruck or the rest of Vermont, save for Dr. Dan. And she only knew him via the short-term rental app she'd used to secure her half of the duplex. She doubted he'd been the one to spill the beans and broadcast the news of her arrival from LA. He clearly didn't seem like the type to start a holiday movie frenzy. How had he so succinctly put it?

I don't even like *Christmas.*

He'd certainly seemed serious. Gross. Who *bragged* about being a Grinch?

The Grinch himself, that's who.

Candy shuddered as she stepped outside the cute Victorian and checked to see if the coast was clear. The good doctor (snort) must be at work, because his windows were dark and there was nary a wiry green Grinch hair in sight. Excellent. She could take Faith for a walk downtown and pick up some Christmas lights for her half of the porch and yard. The unadorned state of the opposite half no longer seemed like an oversight, but that was Dr. Dan's business.

Candy had promised Faith a perfect first Christmas, and she aimed to deliver. She hadn't come all this way to occupy the only undecorated lot in the entire town. What her landlord did—or, more accurately, *didn't*—do to his half of the property was his business.

There was nothing in her rental agreement that said she couldn't put up decorations. Candy was certain of it. After the gazebo encounter, she'd waited until Dr. Dan was safely out of sight and then she'd slinked back to the Victorian and checked.

Although if Dr. Dan was so Grinch-like, then why had he been wearing that ridiculous reindeer tie? And why did his office look like something out of a porcelain collectibles Christmas village?

What did either of those things matter, though? The obvious hypocrisy of her neighbor's lack of Christmas cheer was none of her concern.

But why did he have to be her landlord? And why, oh why, did she have to imply that he was movie-star-level handsome?

Probably because he is.

Faith's stroller hit a bump in the sidewalk, jostling the sleeping baby ever so slightly. It was enough of a jolt, though, to drag Candy's thoughts away from Dr. Dan and back to the present. She needed to focus. Today was about Faith and her first Christmas, nothing and nobody else.

The Bean was at the end of the street, beckoning Candy with its promise of peppermint blended with rich espresso and sweet cream. But a crowd of moms dressed in yoga pants and puffer coats was gathered at the entrance, along with their gaggle of toddlers and small children. Was this just a cute small-town coffee ritual or was it an ambush?

Candy didn't know if she could take any more headshots or tap dancing children. Yes, there had been actual *tap dancing* in the gazebo yesterday before Dr. Dan turned up with his leading-actor bone structure, his lush Patrick Dempsey hair and his Rudolph tie. No wonder she'd snapped.

Candy wasn't in the mood to be mobbed by stage mothers, so she ducked her head and turned Faith's stroller into the nearest store. As luck would have it, the shop was Blush Boutique, a whimsically stylish children's store. Its pink-and-white-striped awning was dotted with white bows, and the shop window had white crowns painted above the capital *Bs* in the boutique's name. When Candy walked inside, the first thing she saw was a rack of tiny Christmas clothes, topped with a stunning display of dozens upon dozens of wooden nutcrackers and plush mice toys.

Faith kicked her little legs and let out a happy squeal. Candy plucked one of the mice toys from the display and handed it to her. She grabbed onto it, instantly mesmerized by the mouse's comically huge pink velvet ears.

"You got here just in time. The mouse army is brand-new, and those little guys have been flying off of the shelf all morning," a woman behind the counter said.

She was wearing a sunny yellow, lemon-shaped enamel clip in her hair and looked vaguely familiar, but Candy couldn't quite place her. Two other customers stood at the counter—a brunette in a pencil skirt and stilettos, and a tiny blonde wearing yoga clothes. All three women were sipping from coffee cups emblazoned with the Bean's logo, and the scent of peppermint hung heavy in the air. Candy's caffeine-deprived soul felt a pang of longing.

"Welcome to Blush Boutique. I'm Melanie. Can I interest you in a peppermint mocha?"

The shop owner smiled and gestured toward a large box of coffee on a silver tray, along with a stack of cups from the Bean.

Hallelujah, joy to the world, God bless us everyone. "Yes, please. That would be amazing."

Candy guided Faith's stroller toward the counter. "Unless this is some sort of bribe because you think I can get you, your children or your pet into a holiday movie? Because I can't, I promise."

One of the coffee-sipping customers gasped. "You're Candace Cane, the new visitor from California!"

"I knew it," the other one said.

Seriously? How did *everyone* seem to know who she was? Did Lovestruck have a massive group text chat or something?

"Don't be freaked out. It's a small-town thing. There are no secrets in Lovestruck." Melanie handed her a steaming cup of coffee from the Bean box. "And don't worry. We aren't going to try and worm our way into one of your movies, are we?"

She glanced at the other two women.

"No, we're not," the petite blonde said.

"Nor are we going to force our children onto you." The chic pencil-skirt wearer shrugged one of her elegant shoulders. "Even though they're all completely adorable and dressed in matching Christmas outfits at my aunt's yarn store right now. Aunt Alice and her knitting group are making them stripy Christmas socks this morning."

"Their outfits aren't matchy-matchy. Just sort of matching, like Beyoncé and Destiny's Child." The blonde twirled a finger, indicating their surroundings. "Mainly because they all came from this boutique."

The brunette bit back a smile. "But we can't make any promises on behalf of Diane Foster. She will *definitely* force her kid onto you. Probably her dog and cat as well."

"Duly noted. Also, please call me Candy. Candace is way too formal," Candy said. She liked these women already. She waved a hand at Faith sleeping in the stroller with the mouse tucked against her cherubic face. "And this is Faith. I unexpectedly got the month off and I wanted to bring her someplace where she could experience a real old-fashioned holiday for her first Christmas."

"Then you definitely came to the right place. I'm Madison," the woman said, tossing her thick chestnut hair over her shoulder. Then she gestured with her coffee cup to the petite blonde. "And this is Felicity. We're friends with Melanie, so sometimes we come over to have coffee at Blush."

"It's nice to meet all of you." Candy felt her shoulders fully relax for the first time since her painful gazebo encounter the day before. This was more like it—nice, regular people welcoming her and Faith to town.

Mostly regular, anyway.

"Is that a Miss America crown?" Candy's coffee cup paused halfway to her mouth as her gaze landed on a sparkling tiara encased in a Lucite box next to the cash register.

"Indeed it is. And if you join us for one of our wine nights, Melanie might even let you try it on." Felicity waggled her eyebrows.

So *that's* why the boutique owner looked so familiar. "You're the turn-lemons-into-lemonade Miss America, aren't you?"

"Guilty as charged, although that was quite a while ago." Melanie shrugged. "See? I told you—there are no secrets in Lovestruck."

"Dr. Dan's nurse is a sweetheart, but she likes to talk." Felicity pulled a face. "A lot."

Ah, so the Christmas crocs pediatric nurse had been the one who'd started the audition frenzy. That made sense. She was around kids and their moms all day. Candy probably should have guessed.

"Try not to be mad at her. She means well, and I think she was just excited about the possibility of Lovestruck becoming Hallmark Channel–famous," Madison said.

"I'm not mad. She seemed lovely." Candy's voice dropped to a murmur. "Unlike her employer."

"Wait." Felicity tilted her head. "What did you just say?"

Candy shook her head. When was she going to learn to keep her thoughts to herself? Hadn't she *just* gotten herself into trouble by sticking her foot in her mouth less than twenty-four hours ago? "Never mind. It was nothing."

Too late. Her trio of new friends exchanged an amused glance, and she knew without a doubt that the cat was out of the bag—probably because she'd let it loose herself.

"Every mom in Lovestruck swoons over Dr. Dan. Apparently you got the memo that he's rural Vermont's answer to Dr. McDreamy on *Grey's Anatomy*," Melanie said.

"It's the hair, right?" Felicity sighed. "And those piercing gray eyes."

Well, at least Candy wasn't the only one who'd fallen into a Patrick Dempsey-esque lust spiral at the sight of the man. "Straight out of central casting, except apparently he hates Christmas."

Madison frowned. "That can't be right."

"I just took Nick in for an ear infection last week, and Dan was wearing a snowman tie. It had stick arms poking out of it and everything." Felicity made jazz hands, which Candy assumed were supposed to resemble Frosty the Snowman's twig-like fingers.

Melanie nodded. "He's famous for his themed novelty ties."

"I'm telling you—he dislikes Christmas. He told me so, point-blank." Candy cleared her throat. "Right after I made an idiot out of myself by assuming he wanted to be an extra in a holiday movie."

Felicity winced. "Cringe."

"Yes. It was cringe-worthy times a million, which is why I dread running into him every time I walk out the door of the duplex," Candy said.

Melanie came out from behind the counter to straighten a rack of toddler sweaters. "It's just kind of hard to imagine a hot pediatrician in a snowman tie being anti-holiday."

Madison tossed her empty paper cup in the trash and smoothed down her pencil skirt. "And doesn't Dan volunteer every year at the first aid booth at the Christmas festival?"

Felicity tapped her holly-berry red nails on the sales counter. "Wait a minute, though. His house is the only one in the entire historic district that isn't already covered in Christmas lights."

What with providing medical care to small children and doing volunteer work and all? Candy shifted from one foot to the other. Perhaps she'd been slightly judgmental. A person could dislike Christmas and still be a decent human being, couldn't they?

Nope. She just couldn't wrap her sugarplum-loving head around such a bizarre concept.

"Exactly," she said. "Not a single twinkling bulb. That's actually what I'm doing on Main Street. I wanted to see if I could get a string or two of lights from the hardware store for my half of the duplex. And a cute snowsuit for Faith, if you have one."

Melanie beamed at her. "Oh, I have a huge

selection of precious snowsuits. That's no problem at all."

"Neither are the Christmas lights. The hardware store has an entire aisle of them." Madison
planted her hand on her hip like she meant business. "But if you want to give Faith a real old-
fashioned Christmas, I think you can do better
than just a strand of twinkle lights."

Felicity nodded. "Way better. They've got the
cutest inflatable Rudolph yard decoration. It's
twelve feet tall and its nose lights up."

Candy laughed. Felicity was joking, wasn't
she? "I walked here. There's no way I can drag
a twelve-foot reindeer back home."

"Also not a problem. The firehouse is right
across the street. My husband, Wade, can give
us a ride back to your place in the fire department's SUV." Felicity was already reaching for
her coat, ready to go hunt inflatable reindeer.
"Madison and I will come along."

"Absolutely," Madison said.

Melanie had already begun lining up a selection of infant snowsuits on the sales counter. There was every shade of pink imaginable,
but Candy was drawn to the puffy, Christmas-
themed ones. Because of course she was.

Joy bubbled inside her. For the first time

since she'd left the gazebo the night before, she felt like perhaps packing up and flying to Vermont hadn't been an impulsive mistake.

Was this how things worked in a small town at Christmas? People who didn't have acting aspirations or a nonsensical dislike of the holidays bent over backward to welcome you, and relative strangers offered you the use of an emergency vehicle to transport oversize reindeer?

If so, Candy approved. This was just like a holiday movie—maybe even better.

Madison was right. She and Faith had definitely come to the right place, Dr. Dan Manning and his performative wearing of snowman ties notwithstanding.

Dan saw the shadow looming over his street the second he rounded the corner from Main Street onto Maple Drive. It was as if the Goodyear blimp had parked directly overhead. Or possibly one of those huge floats from the Macy's Thanksgiving Day Parade that his mom always insisted on watching every year while stuffing the turkey.

Dan had nothing against the Macy's parade, per se. Who didn't love watching a sixty-foot turkey bob and float its way down Park

Avenue? He just opted to leave the room before Santa rolled onscreen in his horse-drawn sleigh. Or worse, when the Rockettes showed up in their illuminated antlers and brown velvet bodysuits, pawing and prancing like reindeer.

Just thinking about it made Dan's eyes roll so hard that they almost fell out of his head and barreled all the way back to Main Street. Regardless, he was seriously beginning to wonder about the shadow. He glanced up, expecting to see a dark cloud, swollen with snow, hanging above the curve up ahead where his house sat. Nothing. The sky was as clear as could be, not a flurry in sight.

Yesterday's snow still covered the ground, and Dan passed no fewer than three snowmen as he walked the two blocks from Main Street to the bend in the road. One of them had a fuzzy navy blue scarf wrapped around its frozen neck—a flagrant abuse of fine cashmere, by all appearances. People lost their minds in Lovestruck this time of year. He was counting down the days until January. *Literally.* Every day of December that passed got crossed out with a black *X* on the calendar that was pinned to his refrigerator with a Lovestruck Maple Syrup Fest magnet.

His fingertips twitched just thinking about marking off today's little square with two swipes of his Sharpie. But then the sidewalk curved, and he caught his first glimpse of the object that was casting its mammoth shadow on Maple Drive.

He stopped dead in his tracks. One of his neighbors had set up an inflatable reindeer of King Kong–sized proportions in their yard. It was so large that its bobbing red-nosed head was even with the pitched roofs of the Victorian cottages that lined either side of the street. Rudolph's antlers completely cleared the round turret on the Williamses' home, directly next door to Dan.

Or was that *his* turret?

Dan started walking again, his horror growing with each step. That *was* his turret, and the enormous inflatable monstrosity was standing in *his* yard.

There had to be some sort of mistake. Clearly. Maybe one of his neighbors had hired a team to install the thing and they'd placed it in front of the wrong house. Or maybe it was some sort of awful practical joke. Dan was friends with the guys on the LFD, and they had a reputation for being jokesters.

But *this*… This was not at all funny. It was horrendous. And it wasn't until he stood directly in front of his tasteful blue duplex that he noticed that half of the house was also covered in crisscrossing strands of Christmas lights— not white, but multicolored. Matching wreaths hung on the duplex's doors, and the white columns on the porch were wrapped with red velvet ribbons. Dan glanced around, half expecting Clark Griswold to jump out from behind one of the reindeer's haunches.

But no, this wasn't the work of that nut from *National Lampoon's Christmas Vacation*. Dan's porch columns now looked like peppermint sticks, which could only mean one thing— Candy Cane had worked her Hollywood magic on *his* property. She'd turned his home into the real estate equivalent of an ugly Christmas sweater.

A small crowd began to gather on the sidewalk across the street. Teenagers snapped selfies with the oversize reindeer towering in the background, like it was a dinosaur from *Jurassic Park*. Dan seethed.

This wasn't happening. He had to get rid of this thing before a photographer from the

Lovestruck Bee showed up and his home landed on the newspaper's front page.

He stalked toward the door on the rental side of the duplex and pounded on it. The wreath shook like a frightened Chihuahua.

Then the door swung open and there stood Candy, dressed in jeans with a hole in the knee, a furry white Angora sweater and a Santa hat. The smell of freshly baked chocolate chip cookies wafted from inside the house. It was like being slapped in the face by Christmas Past.

Something stirred deep inside him.

"Hi," Candy said. Her cheeks were as pink as the roses that bloomed on either side of Main Street in high summer. "Can I help you with something?"

Dan snorted. Was she seriously going to pretend that Santa's tenth reindeer, Godzilla, wasn't looming directly behind him? "Yes, as a matter of fact. You can help me with this."

He waved a hand toward his yard, which now resembled a North Pole–themed fun park. Minus the fun.

"Don't you love it?" Her eyes lit up. "You're welcome."

She flashed him a wink.

It was the smallest possible flutter of her eyelashes, but the wink floated through him like a snowflake. Crystalline and luminous. Utterly unique.

Dan swallowed. Hard. He could *not* be attracted to a woman named Candy Cane…especially *this* woman. "I don't love it. Quite the opposite. In fact, I need you to deflate it right now and take it back to wherever it came from."

Her smile widened. "Sorry, but no. Merry Christmas, though. Thanks for stopping by."

She moved to close the door, and Dan held up a hand to stop it. It thwacked against his palm with a thud.

"Look, I hate to pull the landlord card. You've already paid your rent for the month in full and I want you to enjoy your time in Lovestruck." Did he, though? Did he really? Right now, not so much. "But it's my duplex, my yard and my astronomical electricity bill."

"It's also *your* rental agreement, and I went over it with a fine-toothed comb last night. There's nothing in it prohibiting Christmas decorations." She shrugged, and that furry sweater of hers slipped off one shoulder, exposing a tantalizing glimpse of soft, creamy skin. "Not one word."

Of course there wasn't. Who in their right

mind spent time or money on outdoor decorations for someone else's yard? The triple-XL version of Rudolph must have cost a fortune. Candy was in show business, though. She probably had money to burn, and if Dan wasn't careful, she might try to do so with a cozy Christmas bonfire in the middle of his yard.

"There's definitely a nuisance clause," he countered. "And this—" he cut a glare toward the reindeer "—is certainly a nuisance."

Candy crossed her arms. Her lips pursed, and Dan couldn't help but notice that her mouth looked like a perfect red bow on a holiday package, just waiting to be unwrapped. "You can't be serious. It's *Christmas*. I kept everything on my side of the yard, and I stopped short of putting a lump of coal on your welcome mat. You should be thrilled."

Dan's gaze flicked toward his door. "No lump of coal, but you got me a wreath instead."

It hung there in all its holiday glory, with red berries and pine cones that had been dipped in silver glitter to look like snow. The perfectly matched partner to the wreath on Candy's door.

"It was a gift." Candy's smile wobbled, sending a stab of shame straight through Dan's chest. The wreath would have been a nice gesture, he supposed, if not for the accompanying blinking lights and blow-up doll. "I don't know what I was thinking."

He could hear his mother's voice in the back of his head, telling him to say thank you. But that would only encourage her.

"Clearly we disagree on the aesthetics of a twelve-foot inflatable animal. Regardless, it's a nuisance. This house is over one hundred years old. The circuit breaker can't handle this madness." Dan jammed a hand through his hair, tugging hard at the ends and wishing he was back at the office extracting popcorn kernels from toddlers' nostrils or being vomited on. Anything but this.

"It's fine. It's *been* fine for hours now." Candy rolled her eyes. "You shouldn't lie like that. It's a good way to end up on Santa's naughty list."

Honey, I am *Santa's naughty list.*

Dan glared at her, forbidding himself from saying it out loud. The last thing he wanted— or needed—was Candy Cane trying to reform him. There wasn't a chance of his heart growing three sizes on Christmas morning. Besides, it wasn't as if he was a thoroughly terrible person the other eleven months of the year.

Just this one.

"I'm not lying," he said with exaggerated calm.

"Oh, please." Candy's eyes danced, as if she enjoyed tormenting him. Maybe she did. Maybe he enjoyed it too…just the smallest possible amount. "As Buddy the Elf once said to the department store Santa, 'you sit on a throne of lies.'"

Dan almost smiled, and just as he caught himself, a sizzling noise pierced the strange tension between them. The lights in the interior of the duplex behind Candy flickered before going completely dark. The fan powering Godzilla the reindeer sputtered and then stopped. Dan ducked for cover as the giant animal swayed and then began to slowly deflate, but not before a puffy antler sent him colliding into Candy.

His hands closed into fists around her impossibly soft sweater. She smelled like sugarplums and royal icing—like Christmas itself.

Dan's breath clogged in his throat.

When she spoke, her voice hummed through him with enough electricity to power an entire herd of inflatable caribou. "Son of a nutcracker."

Chapter Four

Candy lay in bed the following morning, savoring the few quiet moments she usually had before Faith began stirring in her crib.

At four months old, baby Faith already slept through the night—thank goodness. And if Candy had been a normal person, she would have kept her eyes clamped shut until the last possible second, so she could get some rest.

But Candy wasn't normal. She was in show business. She'd grown accustomed to the late nights and early mornings that came with set life a long, long time ago. Try as she might, she just couldn't sleep past 5:00 a.m. Under ordinary circumstances, being an early riser gave her plenty of time to go over the call sheets and familiarize herself with what scenes they'd be shooting that day.

There was nothing ordinary about Candy's current circumstances, though. She was a mom now, which she loved. And she was on vacation, which she loathed.

The minute her eyes fluttered open and she saw in the morning glow from the nearby street lamps delicate snow flurries doing a pitter-patter dance against the windowpane, confirming that she wasn't anywhere near Los Angeles, Candy rolled over and screamed into her pillow. It was time to face the truth—she was two and half days into her "perfect Christmas vacation," and thus far, things weren't so perfect. Save for making a few new friends the day before, things were actually pretty terrible.

Creating nostalgic family moments onscreen was easy. Candy had been doing it for years, but thus far, mustering up that same sort of holiday magic in real life instead of on a sound stage was proving to be a bit more challenging.

Was it weird that she wanted to blame her cranky landlord? Every time he was around, things seemed to go haywire. The Great Gazebo Holiday Humiliation—which definitely would have been the title if Candy was living in a movie—had only been the beginning. Just after getting her half of the duplex's exterior practically picture-perfect, Dr. Dan came knocking on her door and *boom*—out went the lights. Down went her adorable twelve-foot reindeer. Splat went her heart, right at her feet.

It didn't help that she'd just failed so horrendously at baking a simple batch of chocolate chip cookies that she'd dumped the batter straight into the trash and resorted to eating half a bag of Chips Ahoy and lighting a cookie-scented candle from Bath & Body Works instead. Candy hadn't even been able to keep that particular humiliation private, since Dan had been forced to enter her half of the premises to replace her blown fuses.

She'd been forced to watch him loosen another cute novelty tie and roll up his sleeves, heart pounding at the sight of his manly forearms. His stomach had growled like mad while his head was stuck inside the fuse box. When he'd emerged with mussed hair that looked like he'd just climbed out of bed and asked if he could possibly have a cookie—given that her house smelled like each and every one of the Keebler elves lived there—Candy had the insane desire to run to the kitchen and attempt another batch. But then Dan had laughed when she'd fessed up about the candle, and not just a polite little chuckle. It had been a full-on guffaw, especially once she'd been forced to ask him how to reset the smoke detector. She'd wanted to strangle him with her apron strings right then and there.

Candy lifted her head from the pillow, rolled onto her back and sighed. She would *not* let the Grinch next door ruin her holiday. There were still three weeks left of December. Surely she could whip up a decent batch of cookies or cobble together a gingerbread house during that amount of time. She'd make sure of it. If necessary, she'd become an excellent holiday baker purely out of spite.

She threw off the covers and walked straight for her robe and slippers. Then she checked on Faith, still sleeping soundly in her crib. Her tiny chest rose and fell while her rosebud mouth made sweet little suckling sounds. Candy's chest suddenly felt like a tight band had been placed around it, making it difficult to breathe.

She wished she knew more about her cousin,

Faith's birth mother. What was she going to tell the baby about her family when she was old enough to ask questions? At least Candy had been given a chance to get to know her mother and father before the terrible car accident that had taken both their lives shortly after her sixteenth birthday. She could still remember the smell of her mother's perfume, the softness of her arms when she wrapped Candy in a hug. Her father's deep belly laugh still echoed in the back of her head when she thought about the nights they used to sit around the kitchen table eating homemade ice cream sundaes and playing board games as a family. Candy had carefully preserved each and every memory she had of her mom and dad, holding on to them as tight as she possibly could, lest she forget. But Faith wouldn't even have that small luxury.

The sweet baby's eyes fluttered open, searching the strange room in a panic until her gaze landed on Candy.

"I'm right here," Candy whispered as their eyes met and Faith's mouth curved into a smile. As gently as possible, Candy lifted the baby from the crib and snuggled her sleepy form against her shoulder.

Candy's eyes pricked with unshed tears as

she inhaled her soft baby powder scent. She took a deep breath and rocked from side to side. Faith cooed and balled her hands into tiny fists, grabbing onto the collar of Candy's red-and-white-striped Christmas robe.

"I'm here," she whispered against Faith's downy head. "Mommy's here."

That's who she was now—Faith's mommy. Candy was all that Faith had, which was why she had to make this holiday work. The child had lost so much in her short life. She deserved a real family Christmas, like she would have gotten if her parents had still been alive. She deserved baby's first Christmas ornaments and pictures with Santa. A plate of cookies left out on Christmas Eve and a live tree that smelled like evergreen and pine. And it was up to Candy to give her those things now, nobody else.

Making a picture-perfect holiday was the only remotely maternal skill that Candy possessed. Maybe it was a little harder in real life than on camera, but she'd figure it out.

No matter what, or *who*, got in her way.

The waiting room at Dan's medical practice was packed, and either he was imagining things or every patient he saw seemed to have some sort of Christmas-related ailment.

First up was a pair of young twins who'd thought it had been a good idea to duel with peppermint sticks…until one of them ended up with a candy cane in the eye. Then he stitched up an eight-year-old who'd sliced a finger open on a broken ornament while helping his mom decorate their Christmas tree. And of course Diane Foster was back, convinced that little Joey had appendicitis. It had taken Dan half an hour to convince her that Joey's appendix was just fine. He'd simply overindulged on eggnog and Christmas cookies the night before. The kid needed a bottle of Pepto, not surgery.

"Is it just me, or is Christmas taking kids out left and right this year?" Frances said as she handed Dan a medical chart and pointed toward the exam room at the end of the hall. "You've got a kid in room three with an allergic reaction to his ugly sweater."

Dan took the file folder and bit back a smirk. *Right there with you, kid.*

Frances gave him a look that told him she knew exactly what he was thinking. "Don't be so cynical. I don't know who you're trying to fool—everyone in town is talking about your yard."

He looked up from the folder. "What?"

"Your yard." Frances held her arms out wide. Her jingle bell earrings did a noisy little dance. "Gigantic reindeer, rainbow lights, matching wreaths on the doors. Does any of this ring a bell?"

Dan slammed the medical chart closed. "Unfortunately, yes. I've been trying to block it all out. Thanks for the reminder."

When he'd left for work this morning, Rudolph was still in a limp pile on the snowy front yard. With any luck, the deflated reindeer would be gone by the time he headed home today, returned to the hardware store or the North Pole or wherever it had come from.

"That wasn't my doing. It was my tenant," he said.

Frances nodded. "I should have known. For a minute there, I'd thought you'd come around and embraced the spirit of the holidays."

Dan's jaw clenched. He wasn't embracing anything...not even the lovely curves beneath Candy Cane's fuzzy sweaters and frilly Christmas aprons. Although every time he thought about her cookie-scented candle, he couldn't help but smile. Candy wasn't quite the Christmas queen she made herself out to be, was she?

The thought that they might have something in common intrigued him. That alone was a problem, though. Dan didn't want to be intrigued. He just wanted to get through the rest of the month and operate on autopilot until New Year's Day.

"Nothing's changed. It's still business as usual around here," Dan said.

Frances tilted her head. "So I shouldn't tell you that invitations to Christmas parties have been pouring in all day?"

Dan sighed. He'd thought his patients knew the drill by now. He'd declined so many invitations to open houses, potlucks, caroling events and holiday parties through the years that eventually they'd simply stopped coming.

"You're joking," he said flatly.

"Nope." Frances shrugged. "There are at least half a dozen piled on your desk. Your decorated yard really sent a message to the community."

The *wrong* message. Clearly.

"No." Dan shook his head. "No, no, no."

"You've got the saying wrong." Frances's eyes twinkled. "It's *ho ho ho*, not *no no no*."

Dan almost laughed, but caught himself in the nick of time. "Cute, but the answer is still no. I'll have the staff decline them all on my behalf."

"Without even looking at them?" Frances tutted. "You won't know what you're missing. The curiosity alone would kill me if I were you."

"Speaking of your curious streak…" Dan crossed his arms over his latest novelty tie. Today's was covered in red sequins and featured glittering white snowflakes and a unicorn with rainbow-colored mane, which prompted the question: Since when were unicorns in any way holiday-related?

Dan didn't want to know. The tie had been a gift from a patient, so he'd added it to the December rotation without questioning its accuracy.

"You're going to talk to me about boundaries again, aren't you, Doc?" Frances grimaced.

"I'm afraid so, yes." Why did he feel guilty all of a sudden? It was a necessary conversation. "Did you spread the word around town that Ms. Cane is here and that she works in show business?"

Frances's forehead creased, as if she was trying to recall one of the dozens of discussions she'd had about the topic at hand. "Perhaps I maybe told a few people. One…two…"

Dan arched an eyebrow.

"Or ten." The older woman flushed. "But I couldn't help it. It's just so exciting. She's not mad at me, is she?"

At Frances? No.

At Dan? Probably.

"Let's just say she's a lot more upset about her giant reindeer getting taken down than she is about the rumor mill." Dan tucked the file folder under his arm and headed for the exam room with Frances scurrying behind him. "But try and refrain from telling anyone else about her personal business. She's only here on vacation."

"Really? Because a lot of us were hoping she'd make a movie right here in Lovestruck."

"Really. This is Vermont, not la-la land." Even though during the holidays it sometimes seemed like everyone in town was living in a fantasy world.

"I wonder how she ended up here, though." Frances peered up at him. "Don't you?"

Truthfully, yes. Dan did, in fact, wonder how Candy had found herself in Lovestruck, clear across the country from California. Sure, his little town was picturesque at Christmas. But it was also located in the heart of rural Vermont. Not many people knew about their charming dot on the map, least of all bigwig Hollywood people. But that was only the tip of the iceberg. If he was really being honest, Dan wondered quite a few things about his beautiful neighbor.

None of which he had any intention of getting to the bottom of.

"I think it's best if we just give her some privacy." Dan reached for the doorknob of the exam room.

"Got it. I'll keep my lips zipped," Frances said.

I'll believe it when I see it.

"Thank you." Dan turned the knob.

"But—" Frances bit her lip.

Dan released his grip on the knob with a sigh. Hopefully, the ugly Christmas sweater hadn't done too much of a number on his child patient. "But?"

"Well, I'm not sure I should say anything, seeing as you keep telling me to mind my own business," Frances said.

She was baiting him, obviously, and he wasn't going to fall for it. He refused.

Don't do it. Don't ask.

He sighed. "Is it something important?"

Damn it, he'd asked.

Frances shrugged, feigning nonchalance, but Dan could see the twinkle in her eyes. His nurse was enjoying this way too much. "Not unless you consider your own front yard important."

His own yard? What now? Was his snowy lawn playing host to real, live reindeer games all of a sudden? Dan wouldn't be surprised. It seemed like the next step up from a twelve-foot Rudolph.

"Frances." He arched a brow. "What's going on?"

But she had no intention of making things easy on him—not after his criticism, even though he'd made every effort to be gentle.

"Are you sure you want me to tell you? We both know how much you love your boundaries," Frances said with an exaggerated flutter of her eyelashes.

"Just spit it out," he said.

She flashed him a triumphant grin. All hope Dan had of establishing anything remotely resembling boundaries in his office went up in smoke.

"The giant reindeer is back up and running. There are dozens of pictures of it all over Instagram already." Frances fished her phone out of the pocket of her scrubs and held it toward him.

The entire screen was filled with shots of his house, looking like it was about to be trampled by Santa's favorite red-nosed pal. Dan gripped the phone so tight that he worried it might crack in two. He couldn't help it, though. What was going on? Was Candy *trying* to burn his house down? Setting off the smoke detector and blowing a fuse in the same day wasn't enough, so she'd decided to give it another go?

"I guess the guys at the fire department got wind of your fuse situation, so they went over to the hardware store, picked up a portable generator and got it all set up to power the yard decorations." Frances tugged her phone out of his hands. It took three firm yanks, but he finally forced himself to stop gaping at the pictures and let it go. "Wasn't that sweet?"

Ah, the joys of small-town living. In between calls for rescuing kittens in trees, the LFD had time to personally help a tourist with her garish monstrosity of a Christmas decoration.

Sweet.

He blew out another sigh. *Sweet* was one word for it, but not the first adjective that sprang to Dan's mind.

Not by a long shot.

Chapter Five

By the time evening rolled around, Candy had made no progress whatsoever in her quest to transform herself into someone who'd have a shot at being picked for the holiday edition of *The Great British Baking Show*. Or any edition, really. Another batch of cookie dough rested in a tragic lump at the bottom of the kitchen trash can. She'd gotten the amounts for the sugar and flour mixed up. Again. But that was okay... *truly* it was, because Candy's yard decorations were back up and running, thanks to the fire department.

It was the tiniest of triumphs, but Candy would take what she could get. Her holiday and Faith's first Christmas were officially back on track. And now the two of them were on their way to the very first night of the Lovestruck Christmas festival—an honest-to-goodness holiday street fair, just like the ones that Candy had been re-creating for television movies for her entire career.

"I've never been to a real Christmas festival before," she said as she pushed Faith's baby buggy down the sidewalk alongside Felicity and Madison, who were each pushing strollers of their own. Madison's was a special double stroller for her toddler twins, Emma and Ella.

Candy couldn't believe it. She'd suddenly become part of a mom posse. She wondered if either Felicity or Madison could tell that she was completely new at this. Probably...and Candy would eventually share her story with them, but not yet. She just wasn't ready, especially considering how news moved around Lovestruck at the speed of light.

"Wait." Felicity held up a hand. "Never? As in...never *ever*?"

"Not as an adult," Candy corrected. "I went to one a long time ago with my family, but I was only sixteen. It seems like a lifetime ago, honestly."

It *was* a lifetime ago. So much had changed since that long-ago Christmas, but the festival she'd attended that year had been right here in Lovestruck…just a night before her magical winter night at the gazebo. Her breath caught in her throat just thinking about it.

"Surely you've at least been to an outdoor Christmas market. We even had those when I lived in Manhattan. Every December, white tents would pop up in Columbus Circle at the edge of Central Park. Practically the entire city smells like roasted chestnuts this time of year." Madison sighed. "It's just lovely."

"But not as lovely as the Lovestruck Christmas Festival. You're in for a definite treat." Felicity nodded, but then slowed to a stop as they rounded the corner onto Main Street. "Unless you're allergic to camels. You're not, are you?"

"Camels?" Candy's gaze flitted toward the town square, where the festival appeared to be in full swing in a dizzying whirl of twinkle lights, jingle bells and holiday carols just beyond the town Christmas tree. There wasn't a camel in sight.

Then again, Candy only had eyes for the gazebo. It glittered in the distance like a lacy white snowflake against the night sky. She'd dreamed about that gazebo for so many years and now here it was, laden with snow and steeped in a memory so precious that she'd been foolish enough to come all this way over a decade later. What had she expected to find? That the boy she'd known back then was still sitting there, waiting for her after all this time?

Of course not. Candy hadn't come back for him, specifically. She'd come back to Lovestruck because it was the last place she'd felt hopeful and optimistic about her future... the last place she'd felt truly *alive*. Even so, she was still annoyed at Dr. Dan for ruining her long-awaited gazebo moment.

Candy dragged her gaze away from the quaint wooden octagon and the memories that seemed to float around it like snow flurries and refocused on the conversation at hand. "Why would there be camels in Lovestruck?"

"For the living nativity scene." Madison tipped her head toward Felicity. "Which is sort of how Felicity and Wade met last year. They played Mary and Joseph."

Candy gasped. "How *sweet* is that?"

And people tried to say the movies she made

were unrealistic. That was a classic meet-cute—much better than, say, mistaking your Grinchy landlord for a wannabe Christmas movie actor and making an idiot out of yourself in the process.

Candy frowned to herself. Actually, that sounded sort of…perfect. Viewers loved a good enemies-to-lovers story. Not that she and Dan would ever budge from their current positioning on the enemies-to-lovers spectrum. Their status was set in stone. The very prospect of leapfrogging all the way to the opposite end was laughable.

Then why aren't you laughing?

"Are you okay?" Madison peered at her. "You look like you've seen a ghost all of a sudden."

"Oh no. I knew it. You *are* allergic to camels," Felicity said.

Get it together. Why are you even thinking *about Dan right now?*

Other than reveling in the fact that he'd failed to permanently deflate her giant reindeer, Candy had no reason to waste precious headspace on the man.

"Nope." She shook her head hard enough to rattle the image of his handsome face right out of it. Almost, anyway. "To my knowledge, I'm not allergic to camels or any other variety of biblical animal."

"Excellent." Felicity grinned, leaving Candy to wonder just how close she was expected to get to said camels.

Not too close, as it turned out. The living nativity scene was like nothing she'd ever seen in person before, though. Even amid the lights and cheer of the festival, a quiet peace seemed to wrap itself around the makeshift manger and the volunteers playing the parts of the holy family, the wise men and a small collection of shepherds.

There was indeed a camel, along with a donkey and a fair number of sheep. One of the shepherds was accompanied by a Border collie, which didn't seem altogether historically accurate but was cute nonetheless. Candy gathered Faith from the stroller and held the baby in her arms so she could see. Her eyes went wide at the sight of the camel. She kicked her little legs when the dog started barking at the sheep. Bless those sweet animals, they put a lump in Candy's throat.

At last. She pressed a kiss to Faith's baby-soft cheek. *A real, old-fashioned Christmas moment.*

"This is amazing," she whispered to Felicity and Madison. "Thanks so much for inviting us to come along."

"Of course." Felicity bounced one-year-old Nick on her hip. "Wade and Jack, Madison's husband, are on duty at the firehouse. I'm sure Wade and I will bring Nick back and do it all over again as a family, but I just couldn't miss opening night."

"Same," Madison said. "Last year, I think I came to the festival every weekend in December." She bent down to straighten Emma's fuzzy red Christmas beanie.

"What do you want to do next—maybe get some homemade hot chocolate at the Bean's booth or check out the homemade wreaths in the craft area? I need to get one for our door before we leave tonight," Felicity said.

"Actually, I was wondering—" Candy aimed a hopeful grin at her new friends. "Is there a Santa here for the kids? I'd love to get a picture of Faith on Santa's lap."

Santa pictures had been a tradition every year during Candy's childhood. Her mother kept all the photos in silver frames and displayed them on the mantel above the fireplace where the family stockings hung. Pictures of Candy's parents with Santa when they were children were always nestled among those of Candy. She'd loved looking at them when she was a little girl. Unpacking the Santa photos and helping her mom arrange them with swags of evergreen along the rough-hewn mantel had been her favorite part of decorating for the holidays.

As much as she loved the old Santa photos, Candy had been so busy traveling to shoots in recent years that she hadn't set eyes on them in ages...until the day after Gabe fired her. Right after she'd snagged flight reservations to Lovestruck, she'd dragged them out of storage and packed all those silver frames in a rolling carry-on so she could take them along. Now they sat on the mantel in her half of the duplex, ready and waiting for a photo of Faith to be added to the Cane family's favorite Christmas tradition.

"Of course there's a Santa. He's one of the most popular attractions at the festival." Madison pointed in the direction of the gazebo. "Santa's velvet throne is just behind the gazebo, next to the skating pond."

Felicity tucked Nick back into his stroller. "Come on, let's go."

They wove their way through the craft and food stalls, inhaling the rich scents of steaming hot chocolate and fresh gingerbread as they went. Everywhere she looked, Candy spotted booths she wanted to come back and visit, from vendors selling carved wooden blocks for toddlers to toy train sets to hand-milled soaps that smelled of cinnamon, evergreen and hot mulled wine. Madison introduced Candy to her aunt Alice, whose yarn store booth had a line a mile long of people anxious to buy knitted mittens and crocheted Christmas stockings. It took close to half an hour to wind their way past the gazebo, and even as they did, Candy's gaze kept going back to it. A sign with a simple red cross had been stuck into the snow just in front of the gazebo, and through a whirl of flurries, she could just make out someone in a red puffer coat tending to an injured child.

Candy's heart sank. She'd been hoping to try again for a little alone time to reminisce there. Clearly, that wasn't going to happen while the gazebo was serving as a first aid station.

"Oh, no," Madison said. "Look at the line."

Candy turned her back on the gazebo and

took in the queue of adults, children and strollers that snaked from Santa's throne halfway around a frozen pond where skaters glided in circles on skates with shiny silver blades.

"Wow. I guess I'm not the only one who wants a Santa photo." Candy deflated as quickly as a giant reindeer who'd just blown a fuse.

"This is only the first night of the festival. If you don't want to wait in that crazy-long line, there will be plenty of other chances for Faith to visit Santa," Felicity said.

"I hate to say it, but I think you're right. I'm going to wait for another night." Candy tried to tamp down her disappointment. *It's fine. You still have weeks here. Tonight has been great—nowhere near a disaster.*

She nodded to herself. So far, the Christmas festival experience was a definite win. She could check that right off her to-do list of perfect small-town holiday activities.

A couple skated past her, drawing her attention to the ice-covered pond. The man and woman were hand in hand with cherry-red cheeks, and the knit scarves around their necks—which definitely looked like they'd come from Aunt Alice's yarn booth—whipped in the wind. A teenager attempted a wobbly arabesque. A young family inched their way across the surface of the ice in a four-person chain with the parents on either end and two small children in the middle. Candy cocked her head. Was that the Charlie Brown ice-skating music drifting from the overhead speakers?

Frank Capra himself couldn't have directed a sweeter skating scene. True *It's a Wonderful Life*–type stuff.

"Earth to Candy. Are you in a trance right now?" Madison waved a hand in front of her face.

"Sorry." Candy laughed. "I'm mesmerized. Are they really skating on an actual pond?"

Madison and Felicity exchanged an amused glance.

"You've been in Hollywood far too long," Felicity said.

Madison nodded toward a white tent where people were trading their snow boots for rental skates. "Go get yourself a pair and take a spin around the ice."

Candy would have loved nothing more, but there was no way she could strap blades to her feet while trying to juggle an infant. She might be new to parenting, but doing so would have clearly been a disastrous idea.

She glanced down at Faith, blinking up at the Christmas lights from her stroller.

"You and Felicity go," Madison said. "I'll stay here and keep an eye on the kids."

Candy's gaze flitted from Faith to Nick to Emma and Ella. "Four against one? Are you kidding?"

Madison shrugged. "It's nothing. Once you've lived with twins twenty-four/seven, you can handle anything. Two…four…six… It's basically the same."

Candy bit back a smile. "I'm not sure that's how math works."

It wasn't how math worked. Candy was sure of it, but she also wanted to take a spin around the ice. Just once.

Nothing was more Christmassy than skating on an outdoor pond. This type of thing was exactly the reason she'd wanted to spend the holidays in Lovestruck. She wouldn't give Gabe and Brian and whatever terrible editorial decisions Brian was probably making about *her* movie a second thought while she was ice-skating under a starry sky.

Plus Faith was drifting off to sleep in her stroller again. Her bedtime had come and gone.

She'd probably never even know that Candy had left her side.

"Seriously," Felicity said. "Madison is a bona fide parenting expert. Trial by fire and all that. The kids will be fine with her for a little bit."

"I'm convinced." Candy nodded. "But just once or twice around the pond. I've never ice-skated before in my life."

Madison settled herself on a park bench, surrounded by the trio of strollers. "No Christmas festivals, no ice-skating. Not to sound judge-y, but where have you been every year at Christmas?"

"On a film set," Candy said.

It was the truth, but somehow she'd never realized how much real life she was missing while she'd been busy creating holiday memories for her viewing audience. Or maybe she had…and had simply been too afraid to think too much about it. Once she cracked opened the lid on her Pandora's box of memories, there would be no turning back.

"We're doing this." Felicity kissed baby Nick on top of the head and then tugged Candy by the elbow until she let herself be dragged away from Faith.

The line to borrow skates was blessedly short.

Most of the skaters were wearing their own—
again, how adorable was that? Candy would have
no idea where to even buy a pair in LA. Within
minutes, though, she was all tucked into her
pretty white rental skates, laced up and ready
to go.

"I'm so excited," she said, watching as the
other skaters made their way around the pond.
Most of them were holding hands and some
sang along to the Christmas carol playing over
the loudspeakers. Candy felt like she'd just been
plopped into a scene from a Christmas card.
Beside her on one of the park benches at the
pond's edge, Felicity finished tying her laces
with a firm double bow. "Ready?"

"Ready." Felicity stood and started walking
toward the pond on her flashy silver blades with
the grace and balance of an Olympic medalist.

Candy pushed herself off the bench and
immediately plopped back down. *Whoa.* Her
ankles felt a bit more unstable than she'd anticipated, and she hadn't even gotten to the ice yet.

Felicity turned around, clearly expecting to
see Candy right behind her. When she saw her
still sitting on the bench, she floated back toward her. Honest to goodness, that's what it

looked like—she *floated*. How was she managing that?

"Everything okay?" Felicity glanced down at Candy's skates.

"Fine. Just feeling a little wobbly when I stand up." She'd teetered more than she'd actually stood, but Felicity got the point.

"Come on. We'll do it together." Felicity offered her a hand.

Candy placed her mitten-clad palm in hers and let Felicity haul her to her feet. They tiptoed toward the pond together. When they reached the pond's edge, Candy took a deep breath and then all of a sudden, they were gliding across the ice.

Frosty wind kissed her cheeks. Snowflakes whirled in front of her face, and Candy felt a little bit less like Bambi on wobbly legs and almost like she could pass for a Lovestruck skating pond regular…except for the death grip she still had on Felicity's hand.

"What do you think?" Felicity grinned at her. If Candy had cut off the circulation to her fingertips, she had the kindness not to let it show in her expression. "It's easier than it looks, right?"

"I feel like I'm in one of those Dickensian Christmas villages," Candy said.

Felicity laughed. "Surely that's a good thing."

"It's a *wonderful* thing."

How had Bing Crosby so colorfully described a place and a moment like this one in the old Christmas record her mother used to play when she was little? A *whipped cream day…a marshmallow world*.

Candy nodded to herself. That was exactly how she felt—finally, her Lovestruck Christmas experience was living up to all of her expectations. She was on a roll. First the living nativity scene, and now this. Clearly the past few days had been a fluke. She'd simply put her earliest attempts at holiday cheer in her rearview mirror and keep going. This Christmas was going to be perfect…not just for Faith, but for Candy, too. She could *feel* it.

Emboldened once again by her usual holiday cheer, Candy released her hold on Felicity's hand. She kept her arms out, airplane-style, and balanced on her own as they headed into another turn.

"Look! I'm doing it," she said and turned to flash a smile at Felicity.

But her gaze snagged on the gazebo, shining

like a glittering, spun glass ornament against the velvet sky. Dan Manning stood alone in its center, watching her from afar.

The Bing Crosby song Candy had been thinking about earlier started spinning again in her head. Except this time her mind seemed stuck on the part about a *yum yummy world made for sweethearts*, like a skip in a record.

Her mouth went dry, which Candy chalked up to the wind, because it couldn't have anything to do with the fact that her Scroogey landlord appeared to be smiling at her. Not a broad holiday grin, but a tender tug of his lips that sent a swarm of butterflies flitting through her belly like forbidden little snow flurries.

Before she could stop herself, Candy lifted her hand and waved at him. It was just a subtle flick of her red mitten, but enough to throw a serious wrench into her newly acquired ice-skating skills. She windmilled her arms and let out a yelp, but it was too late. Her feet slid out from under her and everything moved in slow motion until she landed on the ice with an excruciating thud.

So much for my whipped cream day, she thought as her vision seemed to go hazy around the edges. Skaters kept moving around her in a dizzy blur as a wave of nausea washed over her. Felicity's face came into view. Her lips were moving, but Candy couldn't seem to make out what she was saying. The words were drowned out by the dull roar in the back of Candy's head.

Her eyes fluttered shut, and then her frosty, frothy marshmallow world went black.

Dan stared into Candy Cane's eyes, searching for visible signs that she'd suffered a concussion. Try as he might, he couldn't see anything beyond her velvety brown irises or her thick, dark eyelashes, fluttering as if he'd just made her swoon—which was a ridiculous notion, given that Candy's fall had occurred half an hour ago and had nothing whatsoever to do with him.

"Hello there, Sleeping Beauty," he said as if it were January instead of December and he was fully out of his annual Christmas funk. As if he and Candy were friends instead of….whatever they actually were.

We're nothing to each other, he reminded himself. *She's your tenant, maybe the most annoying one you've ever had.*

"Dr. Dan?" Candy blinked hard. Then she frowned, as if she was disappointed to find him perched on the edge of the sofa, peering down at her.

He breathed a little easier. At least she finally recognized him, although she seemed far less pleased than she'd been when she'd fought her way back to consciousness on the ice. Back at the pond and for the duration of the ride to the duplex, Candy had been so disoriented that she'd kept repeating the same silly, nonsensical phrases over and over again—mostly various forms of the word yum. *Yum. Yummy. Yummiest.*

Then, out of the blue, she'd called him "sweetheart." That's when Dan had become truly alarmed.

"You can drop the formality," he said as he reached to brush a lock of hair from her eyes and then thought better of it. His hand balled into a fist in his lap. "Just call me Dan."

Everyone in Lovestruck called him Dr. Dan, but somehow it sounded a tad snarky coming out of Candy's mouth, which bothered him more than he cared to admit.

"Okay." She swallowed. "Dan."

Then her gaze flitted from his to face to their surroundings—the slate gray walls, the sleek gas fireplace and the minimalist aesthetic that was no doubt a complete contrast to the frenetic chaos that seemed to surround Candy at any given moment. Dan shuddered to think what her home in California looked like. Given that her first action in her temporary holiday rental had been to stick an enormous eyesore on the front lawn, there was really no telling.

"Where am I?" Her lovely doe eyes went wide in alarm as she scrambled to a sitting position.

"You're at my house. Try not to make any sudden movements," Dan said in his strictest doctor voice—the one he only used when he meant business and there was a post-visit sticker or lollipop on the line for one of his young patients. "You hit your head a little bit ago, and you're sure to be dizzy. I don't want you to pass out again."

It seemed presumptuous to tuck her into bed—even in his rarely used guest bedroom—so Dan had situated her on the sofa in his living room after he'd brought her back to the duplex from the Christmas festival. Felicity had volunteered to keep baby Faith overnight so Candy could get some rest, so it was just the two of them.

Not that an infant would have made an effective chaperone. Or that Dan and Candy even *needed* a chaperone. They were two grown adults. Two adults who didn't even like each other…a fact that had slipped Dan's mind a few times as he'd watched her sleep.

"That's right. I passed out. Should I be in a hospital or something?" Candy's eyes went as big as saucers. Then she cocked her head and took another look around his living room. "Do you realize that you don't have a single Christmas decoration in here?"

For the first time in an hour, Dan allowed himself to relax. He might have even smiled.

Candy's eyes narrowed. "What's so funny?"

Dan glanced at the mantel above his fireplace, blessedly free of stockings or swags of evergreen, and back at Candy. "You must not have a concussion if my lack of Christmas decorations is your most pressing concern right now."

Her cheeks blazed pink. "Is that your official medical opinion?"

"Yes and no." Dan shrugged. "But don't worry. I gave you a pretty full neurological exam when you first woke up at the pond. You seemed fine, particularly when you turned your nose up at the idea of resting here where I could keep an eye on you instead of going home next door."

He'd tried not to take it personally. After all, he wasn't altogether thrilled about having Candy spend the night on his sofa—at least that's what he kept telling himself. It made sense, though. She'd hit the ice pretty hard. She had a nice-sized goose egg on the back of her head as well as a sprained ankle. Dan didn't like the idea of her being alone all night. Not at all.

"Do you remember any of what I just told you? Because if not, we might have a problem." Dan frowned down at her.

"Stop glowering at me like that. I remember. Faith is with Felicity and I'm here, in pseudo-medical jail." She rolled her eyes. "I'm just a little disoriented, that's all. I don't generally wake up in strange men's homes."

Dan cocked an eyebrow. "I'm not that strange."

"Your lack of decorations says otherwise," Candy countered.

"You're fine. Clearly." Dan stood. He needed to get to bed. He had a full slate of patients scheduled the following day. But for some reason, none of that seemed to matter as much as keeping an eye on Candy.

She'd looked so happy out there on the ice.

So free. Dan couldn't remember when he'd last felt that way himself. It had been a long, long time. If ever.

He hadn't even realized he'd been staring until she'd waved at him. His first impulse had been to look away and pretend he hadn't seen her bright red mitten or her beaming face, smiling just for him. Then she'd fallen so spectacularly that he'd practically pulled a hamstring hurdling over the railing of the gazebo in his rush to check and see if she'd cracked her head open.

What was happening to him? Maybe Dan was the one who needed to get his head examined.

"Dr. Dan," Candy said just as he reached the hallway that led to his bedroom.

He turned to face her. She looked so small, lying there on his sofa, tucked beneath a quilt his grandmother had made when he was a kid—the one and only tangible reminder of Dan's childhood. The scents of soot and ash had clung to the quilt for months…years. Sometimes, Dan imagined he could still smell it. Impossible, he knew. It was simply his mind playing tricks on him. It was strange how the human brain worked sometimes.

Dan's problem wasn't his brain, though. It was his heart.

Only in December, he reminded himself. The other eleven months out of the year, he was perfectly fine.

"It's just Dan, remember?" he said.

"Right. Dan." Candy gave him a wobbly smile. "Thank you…" She swallowed and pulled his grandmother's quilt snug around her slender frame. "…for everything."

Dan's heart suddenly felt as if it was being squeezed in a vise. "You're most welcome, Candy Cane."

That name. *Candy Cane.* It almost sounded like an endearment. Dan could practically taste the words on the tip of his tongue, sugary sweet and cool like a mint. A breath of fresh, wholesome holiday air.

The sensation lingered as he walked down the dark hallway toward his bedroom, and for the first December in as long as Dan could remember, he closed his eyes and visions of sugarplums danced in his head.

Chapter Six

Candy woke up the following morning to find Dan leaning over her, studying her as if she were a science experiment. The pounding in the back of her head had subsided, but as she shifted to a sitting position, her ankle practically screamed in protest.

Candy winced into the googly eyes of Dan's reindeer tie.

"Tell me what month it is," Dan demanded.

Candy blinked. "December."

Duh.

Dan stood up straighter. The reindeer's

eyes went round and round. "And what's your name?"

"Candy Cane." She narrowed her gaze at him. "Should I be concerned that you don't know this basic information? I thought I was the one with a potential head injury."

"You are, which is why I need to make sure you're alert and okay before I leave for work." He arched a brow. "Do you know who I am?"

Truthfully? No. He'd been awfully nice to her for the past twelve hours. *So* nice that she'd wondered if perhaps he actually liked her, all evidence from the prior few days notwithstanding. And the look he'd given her last night while she'd been skating—at least the part when she'd been upright—had bordered on dreamy.

But maybe those things were just side effects of her near concussion and they'd never really happened at all, because this morning, he seemed back to his regular scowling, Christmas-hating self.

Will the real Dan Manning please stand up?

"You're my neighbor, landlord, town pediatrician and mortal enemy to inflatable reindeer worldwide," she said.

His lips gave a nearly imperceptible twitch. "Satisfactory."

Who on earth talked like that?

She rolled her eyes. "You're a morning person, I see. Please try and take the enthusiasm down a notch...at least until I've had my coffee."

Dan shrugged into his overcoat—the same one he'd been wearing the other night at the gazebo when she'd tried to tell him he was too handsome to be an extra in a Christmas movie. She should have been immune to his good looks at this point, since beauty came from the inside and everything. There was nothing but a lump of coal where his heart was supposed to be, so there was no reason at all for the way her own heart thumped-thumped in her chest as she watched him smooth down his silly tie. His navy coat brought out the blue flecks in his gray eyes, though. Maybe that was it.

Or maybe he's not as completely Grinch-like as you think he is.

"There's a coffee maker on the kitchen counter and creamer in the refrigerator. Something tells me you don't drink it black," Dan said.

Candy shuddered. "Ew, no. The more sugar and flavored creamer, the better. Preferably something seasonal. It's not peppermint patty creamer, is it? That's my favorite."

She was basically trolling him now. There was no way Dan Manning had a bottle of peppermint patty creamer in his fridge, tucked among all the spinach smoothies and whatever other boring things he probably consumed on a daily basis. Antagonizing him was easy…and *necessary*. She didn't want to be attracted to him. Not even a little bit. Loathing each other was so much less complicated.

He stared down at her, perfect brow furrowing. "Do I seem like the type of person who would have peppermint patty creamer on hand?"

"Not for a hot second," she said.

He almost smiled, but seemed to catch himself and arrange his lips back into a flat, humorless line. Still, Candy thought she spied a dimple in one of his cheeks. That dimple alone would have probably launched a thousand fan clubs if he'd actually been an actor.

"Felicity will be here around nine with Faith. Get some rest until then." He glowered with renewed vigor. "Doctor's orders."

He was awfully bossy, considering he was a pediatrician and she was a fully grown adult. Candy wasn't required to actually do as he said. She could have stood up and limped right back to her side of the duplex. But her ankle hurt and it felt nice being taken care of for a change instead of the other way around. At work, Candy was always making sure the actors on set had everything they needed. As soon as the cameras stopped rolling, they were wrapped in warm coats and offered comfy slippers. Snacks of all varieties were available round the clock for both the cast and crew.

But Candy couldn't remember the last time anyone had offered her a cozy quilt or made sure she had a warm cup of coffee in the morning. It was nice…even in the absence of a smile or her favorite creamer.

"Will do," she said around the embarrassing lump that sprang to her throat. What kind of person got emotional over the simplest act of kindness?

The kind who had to learn to live on her own at the tender age of sixteen.

She swallowed hard. "Have a nice day at work."

Dan blinked at her. "Oh. Right. Thank you."

It looked as if Candy wasn't the only one who wasn't accustomed to being cared for. She smiled to herself as he headed for the door. Before she could hear his car back out of the driveway, she burrowed farther beneath Dan Manning's soft quilt and fell back asleep. When she awoke sometime later, she was amazed she'd been out for so long. Something peaceful about Dan's place must have turned off her early-riser clock.

Felicity showed up right on schedule, just as Candy was sipping on the coffee that Dan had promised her. Flavorless as it was, it still somehow tasted like the best coffee she'd had in ages. Maybe she really should get her head examined.

"You don't have plans this morning, do you?" Felicity asked as Candy limped back to the sofa with Faith balanced on her hip.

"Well, let's see. You already bathed and fed my baby for me. Thanks for that, by the way. I really appreciate the babysitting." She grinned at her new friend. "So no, nothing specific."

Although, she was still intent on doing something Christmassy, sore ankle and all. Her time in Lovestruck seemed to be moving at warp speed.

"Good. You're coming with me," Felicity said.

"Where, exactly?" Candy still needed to get cleaned up and changed. She hadn't even managed to do the walk of shame back to her own rental next door. Something told her there wasn't a soul in Lovestruck who would fail to notice if she ventured out and about in the same ugly Christmas sweater she'd been wearing the night before.

"Main Street Yarn. Madison's aunt Alice is giving a class today on making Christmas stockings. It seemed like something you might enjoy." Felicity shrugged. "You can bring Faith along. Alice and her older friends love to dote on the babies while us moms try and get the hang of knitting and crochet."

Us moms.

Candy still needed to explain to Felicity how Faith had recently come into her life. Not that an explanation was necessary, per se. But if they were going to be friends, *real* friends, she felt like she should open up and share.

An hour later, Candy did just that as she sat at the big, round maple table situated in the center of Main Street Yarn's sales floor, awkwardly jabbing her knitting needles into her tangle of red yarn. She told Felicity, Madison, Melanie, Alice and the handful of other class members all about the unexpected phone call she'd gotten a month ago, letting her know she was now a guardian for her baby cousin. She even told them about being temporarily fired—emphasis on *temporarily*.

Now that Candy thought about it, though, she realized she hadn't heard a word from Gabe or anyone else on set since she'd left Los Angeles. Wrapping a film was always stressful, though. Not to mention editing, sound mixing and cutting a trailer.

Still, a text would have been nice. Candy was still a producer on the project, after all.

Are you, though?

"So you're a brand-new mom—even newer than we realized." Felicity beamed at her.

"Brand-spanking-new." Candy glanced down at her knitting. It looked nothing whatsoever like a stocking. "I honestly have no idea what I'm doing. My mom skills are about on par with my yarn skills."

Alice peered at her over the top of her glasses. "Keep going. Finishing is half the battle, and just think—little Faith will always have that stocking as a reminder of her first Christmas. From where I'm sitting, you're doing a fine job, all around."

"Of course you are," Melanie said.

"You couldn't have chosen a better place to bring Faith for the holidays. If a real, small-town holiday is what you want, there's nowhere better than Lovestruck," the older woman sitting directly next to Alice said. Her Christmas stocking was nearly finished, and it looked as perfectly crafted as if it were hanging from the mantel of Santa's own North Pole cottage.

"How did you hear about our little town, though?" Madison cocked her head. "I didn't realize anyone on the West Coast had ever even heard of Lovestruck."

Felicity glanced up at Madison. "You're slipping into reporter mode again."

"Sorry. Ignore me, Candy." Madison grinned. "We're just glad you found us."

"Actually, this isn't my first time here," Candy said. She'd already given them a basic rundown of her life story. What was the harm in telling them about that long-ago Lovestruck Christmas?

"Really?" Felicity's eyes went wide.

"I spent Christmas here with my family way back when I was a teenager. It was the most magical holiday I'd ever experienced. I've always wanted to come back." Candy fumbled with her yarn. "This is the first time I've actually had the chance."

She'd been too busy creating Christmas to really experience it, and now here she was, making a spectacular mess of things. She had the swollen ankle and tragic-looking stocking to prove it.

"That's so sweet, dear. I hope you're enjoying your time here so far," Alice said.

"Is Lovestruck just like you remember it?" Felicity asked.

At the same time, Madison said, "What was your favorite thing about it back then? What do you remember most? And I swear I'm just making conversation. Whatever you say won't end up on the front page of the *Lovestruck Bee*."

"Um," Candy said. She hadn't considered that Madison might be taking notes. In LA maybe, but not Vermont.

"Unless it's really juicy." Madison waggled her eyebrows.

Felicity gave Madison a playful poke with one of her knitting needles. "Would you stop? You're scaring her."

"I'm only kidding," Madison said, crossing her heart. "I promise. Come on, spill. The way you're looking at me right now, I can tell it really *is* juicy."

"Not juicy, exactly. Just…" *Just the most magical moment of my entire life.*

Candy cleared her throat. It had happened over a decade ago and felt even longer. She'd revisited the memory so many times in the past ten years that she'd probably begun to embellish it in her imagination. The time had definitely come to let it go.

She glanced around the table. Everyone was staring at her, knitting needles frozen midair, waiting for her to finish the story.

"Okay, fine. But it's really not that big of a deal." She let out a breath. "I was sixteen, and I was here with my parents. They wanted to take a family vacation someplace snowy for the holidays and had heard about Lovestruck from an old family friend. We spent the entire week here, doing all sorts of Christmassy things, but it never snowed. Not a flake in the sky."

"That's weird. It snows half the year here," Madison said.

Melanie nodded. "This year it even snowed on Halloween."

"Everyone in town was talking about how it was going to be the first time in Lovestruck's history that there wasn't going to be a white Christmas. It was the chatter in every shop, every café and every booth at the Christmas festival," Candy said.

"I remember that year!" Alice grinned.

Felicity glanced at Alice. "Did it at least snow on Christmas Day?"

Alice flashed her a wink. "Why don't we let Candy finish her story?"

Candy took a deep breath. "This is going to sound sort of crazy, but there was a boy that I'd seen on and off all week at the Christmas festivities. We never spoke. Every time I saw him, I was with my parents and he seemed to be on vacation with his family as well. I mean, we were kids."

Candy shrugged, laughing at the memory, even as her cheeks grew warm remembering how breathless she felt every time she'd bumped into him. The secret glances. The quiet smiles…

"And then late on Christmas Eve, I left our B&B and went outside to shoot some video of the town square. I fancied myself a filmmaker, even back then. The streets were completely quiet. Everyone was tucked inside somewhere, spending the holiday with their family. I walked up and down Main Street, capturing little details with my camera until I got to the gazebo… and there he was."

Felicity leaned forward, eyes wide. "The boy?"

"Yep. He was right there, all alone. Just sitting there, as if he'd been waiting for me to find him." Candy's face went hot. These women probably thought she was pathetic. Who still got moony over something that had happened to them when they were just a teenager?

"Keep going," Felicity prompted. "You're killing me here."

"Did you talk to him?" Madison asked.

Candy shook her head. "Strangely enough, we didn't."

Felicity's brow furrowed. "I don't get it. If you didn't talk to him, what happened, exactly?"

"I sat beside him on the bench inside the gazebo and before either of us could say anything, it started to snow." Candy felt herself smile so wide that her cheeks ached.

Melanie's hand flew to her heart. "Oh, my. How romantic."

"It was." Candy shook her head. "I can't even describe how lovely it was—the delicate snowflakes against the night sky, the way we both noticed them at the same time. It was just… magical. Then we looked at each other, and before I could stop myself, I threw my arms around the boy's neck and kissed him right on the lips."

"Oh. My. Gosh. This is the *sweetest* story ever," Felicity said.

Madison nodded. "It's like something out of a Christmas movie."

"It is, isn't it?" Candy sighed. "I think, in a way, I've been trying to re-create that memory ever since. It was so pure, so innocent… I can't remember feeling so full of joy or hope as I did in that moment."

"Surely you found out the boy's name. What happened after you kissed him?" Melanie said.

"I ran away." Candy laughed. "It was my very first kiss. What can I say? I got caught up in the moment of my first white Christmas and went a little nuts. I couldn't believe what I'd done. We kissed for a long time and then I just dashed off, quicker than one of Santa's reindeer."

She looked down at her knitting, doing her best to pretend that leaving hadn't been the biggest regret of her life. Ah, the ignorance of youth. Candy hadn't realized how special the moment had been until she'd been foolish enough to let it slip right through her fingers.

Felicity gasped. "That's why you're here, isn't it? You're looking for him."

Candy's gaze flew to meet hers. "What? Don't be ridiculous."

"You are, aren't you?" Madison groaned. "Ugh, I knew it was going to be juicy. I can't believe I promised not to write about it."

Felicity clapped her hands, as giddy as a kid about to give Santa her Christmas wish list. "You could totally do a story on this. If you did, you might even find the boy!"

Candy shook her head. She knew she shouldn't have told them the story. "Absolutely not. Aren't you forgetting something? Whoever he is, he's not a boy anymore. He's probably married with kids by now. And I'm pretty certain his family was in Lovestruck on vacation. There's no way he lives here."

"Aren't *you* forgetting something?" Felicity raised her brows. "Christmas is the time for miracles. Isn't that the theme of all those movies you make?"

She had her there.

"Those movies are fiction," Candy said quietly. Her smile felt frozen in place.

If anyone knew how far those stories were from real life, it was Candy. That magical

Lovestruck Christmas had been the last one she'd spent with her parents. She knew life wasn't like the movies, and she certainly hadn't come back to Lovestruck expecting to find the boy. She wasn't even looking for him.

The thing she most wanted to find was the magic of the holidays, the belief that anything was possible—any life, any love, any winsome Christmas wish. Candy had been holding on to that perfect Christmas in her heart for a decade, clinging as tightly as she could to the past. But deep, deep down, she wasn't sure she believed anymore.

Not really.

She wanted to… Oh, how she wanted to. How was she supposed to nurture that belief in Faith when she'd lost it herself?

"Hey, are you okay?" Felicity reached over and squeezed Candy's hand. "You look really sad all of a sudden."

"I'm fine," she lied. "Just getting a little misty-eyed thinking about the past. Can we talk about something else now?"

"Of course, dear," Alice said, but her gaze seemed to linger on Candy for the rest of the class.

And in response, Candy did what she always

did. She pasted a jolly smile on her face and threw herself into holiday cheer.

Fake it till you make it. It was Candy's life-long mantra. On the outside, she was Suzy Christmas—wearer of ugly sweaters, singer of carols, creator of holiday stories that never failed to melt the coldest of hearts.

But on the inside, she was still a lost, lonely girl, wishing for yesterday and wondering if the future would ever live up to the past. And as she put the finishing touches on her comically awful Christmas stocking, two questions swirled in the back of her mind...

What would Dan Manning say if he knew it was all an act? But most pressing of all, when had his opinion started to matter?

Chapter Seven

Dan's day was once again filled with trying to fix holiday mishaps in the lives of his young patients. He'd already dealt with two fruitcake-related stomach aches and an allergic reaction to a blue spruce tree by the time a frantic mom came rushing into the clinic with a toddler who'd just eaten a Christmas light.

"What do you mean, he ate it?" Dan said, certain Frances was exaggerating.

"He put it in his mouth, chewed it up and swallowed it," she said. "Some of it, anyway. I gloved up and fished around in his little mouth.

I scooped out some bits of glass, but probably not a whole bulb's worth. The kid might have swallowed a sliver or two of glass."

Dan rubbed his temples. It was official—the holidays were going to be the death of him. But his patients were going to survive the madness. He'd make certain of it.

He went straight to the Christmas light eater's exam room, where the child seemed completely fine. The mother, not so much. Dan wished he could prescribe the poor woman some Xanax, but the best he could do was to send her to the closest ER to get the kid an X-ray, just to be on the safe side.

"Can I interest you in some eggnog?" Frances said when he emerged. "There's a pitcher of it in the break room. Kimberly made it from scratch."

Kimberly, Dan's receptionist, was a perpetual ray of sunshine. She was also a gourmet cook. If she'd made the eggnog, it was certain to be delicious. But alas, it was still eggnog.

Dan declined on principle. "Thanks, but no thanks."

Frances let out a huff. "Suit yourself, Ebenezer. Your loss."

He arched an eyebrow.

"I mean your loss, *boss*." She gave him a saccharine smile and handed him a stack of phone messages written on pink pages from an old-fashioned *while you were out* pad. Tradition ruled the day in Lovestruck, even when it came to office supplies. "Better?"

"Marginally," Dan muttered as he flipped through the phone messages. When the one he was looking for didn't appear, he flipped through them again.

"Expecting a call?" Frances asked.

"No," he said automatically. "Well, maybe. I thought perhaps Candy would have checked in. She sprained her ankle last night at the Christmas festival and I looked after her."

Frances narrowed her gaze at him. "That was awfully nice of you. I take back the Scrooge reference."

"Too late. It's already out there," Dan said, reminding himself that he should feel relieved that Candy hadn't tried to contact him. Why should she, unless she wasn't feeling well?

He'd done his job. He'd patched her up, and now she could go back to her side of the duplex and revel in Christmas cheer while he... did what? Plotted how to steal her roast beast like the Grinch?

"You got another invitation for a holiday party," Frances said, dragging Dan's attention back to work and his actual patients instead of his pretty, albeit slightly clumsy, neighbor.

Candy was a terrible skater, but that hadn't mattered, had it? She'd been having the time of her life. Dan smiled to himself just thinking about her giddy expression when she'd waved to him.

Frances jammed her hand on her hips. "What's that smile for? Don't tell me it's a yes this time. I just told Kimberly to call the fire department and decline on your behalf."

"Sorry." Dan rearranged his lips into a flat, expressionless line. "No, I…wait. Why would she call the fire department?"

"Because it's their party. Cap McBride is hosting a big holiday shindig at the fire station in a few days for all of Lovestruck's first responders. Since you're the town doctor on call once a week and since you volunteer every year at the Christmas festival, you're on the guest list." Frances sighed. "It sounds lovely. Too bad you'll miss it."

"I'll go," Dan said.

The medical chart in Frances's hands slipped

from her fingertips. Dan caught it just before it hit the floor.

"Sorry," Frances said as he handed it back to her. "I must have heard wrong. Either that, or Kimberly must have spiked her eggnog, because I could have sworn you just said you wanted to go to the fire department's holiday party."

"You didn't hear wrong. I'll be there."

Frances tilted her head. "But I thought…"

"If it's for the fire department, I'll do it," Dan said.

"Okay. I'll just go tell Kimberly to change that RSVP." Frances took a single step toward the lobby and then lingered, looking him up and down.

Here it comes.

"Just out of curiosity, is there any particular reason you're making an exception for the fire department?" Frances asked, tone infused with an innocence that Dan didn't buy for a second.

He shot her a weary look. "Boundaries, Frances. Remember?"

"Right." She nodded. "Boundaries. Gotta love them."

Dan just smiled and pretended he believed her, as if he didn't know that Frances would rather swallow an entire string of Christmas lights than respect his personal boundaries.

To his great relief, the rest of the day seemed somewhat normal—stomach flus, sore throats and ear infections ruled the afternoon. It almost seemed like a normal month...

Until Dan came home to find a gift bag hanging from the doorknob of his half of the residence. He almost didn't notice it, distracted as he was by the whir of Rudolph's generator and the reindeer in his yard that looked like it would have been more at home on the set of a *Jurassic Park* movie than at the North Pole. Was he really going to have to look at that thing until the twenty-fifth?

He snatched the gift bag from the doorknob and turned it over in his hands. It didn't have a tag, so there was no telling where it had come from. The community at large showered Dan with Christmas presents every year. He had enough ceramic World's Best Doctor mugs to open his own coffee shop if he ever decided to retire from medicine and end the Bean's monopoly in Lovestruck.

Gifts typically arrived at his office, though. He couldn't remember the last time anyone had dropped one off on his doorstep.

Curiosity got the best of him and he peeked inside the bag before he entered the house. A lump of tangled red yarn rested on a nest of tissue paper.

"What the—" he muttered as he lifted the mystery item from the bag. It unspooled into a long, wonky strip of uneven knitting. Or was that crochet? Or, possibly, just a series of knots?

Dan had no idea what he was looking at, but dread pooled in his gut as he considered that the gift might be a necktie. Lord help him if he was going to have to add this festive eyesore to his rotation of Christmas ties. He'd rather wear a Santa hat every day of the month than walk around with this thing hanging from his shirt collar.

"It's a stocking," he heard someone say in an offensively cheery tone behind him.

Candy.

Of course.

Dan turned to find her standing on the threshold to her half of the house. Clearly he hadn't heard her door open. There was a hiking boot on her left foot, and on her right, the orthopedic air walker he'd strapped onto her sprained ankle the night before. Beneath both feet was a new welcome mat that said "Every time a doorbell rings, an angel gets its wings" in swirly white script.

Dan let his gaze travel upward until it came to rest on her beaming face. Her smile seemed to burrow deep inside his chest somehow. Dan felt warm all over, as if he was standing in front of a crackling fire on a cold winter night. He had the ridiculous notion to invite her inside for s'mores.

"It's a Christmas stocking," she repeated, motioning toward the wad of knitting in his hand.

Dan held it up and glanced from Candy to the red yarn and back again.

Candy winced. "It's terrible, I know. I only learned how to knit this morning. If it's any consolation, the one I made for Faith is even uglier."

"It's not ugly," Dan somehow managed to say with a straight face. "It's…charming."

Candy's eyes sparkled. "Oh, I'm so glad you like it! I just wanted to give you a little something as a thank-you for taking care of me last night."

"That really wasn't necessary." *Truly, it wasn't*, he thought. Although, the fact that she'd made him something was awfully sweet.

"On the contrary, it was super necessary. I've seen your living room, remember? At least now you've got something festive for your mantel." Her gaze flitted to the stocking, and her smile dimmed. "Although, I have to admit, it seemed like less of a mess when I wrapped it earlier. If you don't want to hang it up, I'll understand."

"It's going right up on my mantel," Dan said. Better there than dangling from his neck.

Also, if he didn't put the stocking to good use, she might try and make him something else—like cookies, and the last time she'd tried to bake something, she'd nearly burned his house down.

Never mind the fact that he'd never hung a stocking from his mantel in his entire adult life.

"Excellent," she said, and her smile went megawatt again. "Well…have a nice evening."

She reached for her doorknob, and Dan was once again within seconds of sitting in front of Netflix and ordering pizza—alone, just like he'd done nearly every night of December thus far.

He looked down at the knitted stocking and closed his fingers around the soft red yarn. "How are you feeling? Better, I hope?"

Candy turned to face him. "Oh. Yes, better, thanks. My head feels fine, actually. I was going to take Faith to the festival tonight to try and get her picture taken with Santa, but I thought I should probably rest my foot for a bit. I'm just going to whip up some dinner first and then settle in for a Christmas movie."

"Glad to hear it." Dan nodded. "If you need any ibuprofen or anything, I'm right next door. Unless…"

Unless you want to join me for pizza and a non-holiday-themed binge-watch?

He let his voice drift off. What he was about to suggest sounded an awful lot like a date, and he couldn't date Candy. Absolutely not. She was his tenant. His next-door neighbor. In a way, she was even his patient.

Sort of.

You're blaming your hesitation on an ankle sprain? Really?

Dan's jaw clenched. He couldn't do this. He could *not* let himself get emotionally involved with a woman who seemed like she might be the angel on top of a Christmas tree, all come to life and ready to help him discover the true meaning of the holiday season.

"Unless?" Candy bit her bottom lip, drawing

every bit of Dan's attention to her mouth—red and soft, like a perfect satin Christmas bow.

"Unless…" he said, spellbound.

Was it really such a crazy notion that he might be attracted to Candy Cane? It was only pizza and Netflix, not a marriage proposal.

But before Dan had a chance to pop the question, the wail of a baby pierced the air.

Candy's hand flew to her throat. "Sorry! That's Faith. She must have woken up from her afternoon nap. I should go."

"Of course." Dan took a backward step toward the safety of his own, nondecorated side of the duplex. "You two have a nice night."

"You, too." Candy gave him a flippy little wave and dashed inside.

Dan took a deep inhale of snowy air and blew it out in a puff of vapor and frost. He glanced down at the Christmas stocking, still clutched tightly in his hand, and ran the pad of his thumb over the uneven stitches. It was one of the ugliest gifts anyone had ever given him, which was really saying something, considering Dan had an entire drawer full of macaroni necklaces back at his office.

Still, he couldn't help but smile.

Then he glanced back up and his gaze collided with the inflatable reindeer's gigantic blue eyes. Its huge head bobbed up and down as it came perilously close to wiping out one of the sugar maple saplings Dan had planted last spring.

Dan scowled. "What are you looking at, Rudolph?"

Again, the reindeer's head bobbed up and down. If Dan didn't know better, he might have thought an inanimate lawn decoration was having a laugh at his expense.

You're losing it, my friend. You're letting Christmas get inside your head.

Now if he could just stop himself from letting Candy Cane worm her way into his heart. Something told Dan that might be easier said than done. Surely he could hold out until Christmas, though. It was right around the corner. And then once New Year's Day had come and gone, Candy would head back to LA, he could flip the calendar to January and life would go back to normal.

Dan waited for the impending sense of relief to wash over him, but weirdly, it never did. The emptiness he felt deep in his chest every December seemed more bottomless than ever,

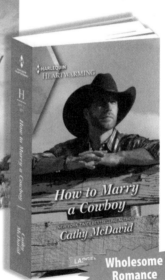

Get up to 4
FREE FABULOUS BOOKS
You Love!

To thank you for being a loyal reader we'd like to send you up to 4 FREE BOOKS, absolutely free.

Just write "YES" on the Loyal Reader Voucher and we'll send you up to 4 Free Books and Free Mystery Gifts, altogether worth over $20, as a way of saying thank you for being a loyal reader.

Try **Harlequin® Special Edition** books featuring comfort and strength in the support of loved ones and enjoying the journey no matter what life throws your way.

Try **Harlequin® Heartwarming™ Larger-Print** books featuring uplifting stories where the bonds of friendship, family and community unite.

Or **TRY BOTH!**

We are so glad you love the books as much as we do and can't wait to send you great new books.

So don't miss out, return your Loyal Reader Voucher Today!

Pam Powers

LOYAL READER
FREE BOOKS VOUCHER

▲ If offer card is missing write to: Harlequin Reader Service, P.O. Box 1341, Buffalo, NY 14240-8531 or visit www.ReaderService.com ▲

BUSINESS REPLY MAIL
FIRST-CLASS MAIL   PERMIT NO. 717   BUFFALO, NY

POSTAGE WILL BE PAID BY ADDRESSEE

HARLEQUIN READER SERVICE
PO BOX 1341
BUFFALO NY 14240-8571

NO POSTAGE
NECESSARY
IF MAILED
IN THE
UNITED STATES

so he shoved the stocking back inside the gift bag, marched inside and slammed the door in Rudolph's smug face.

Chapter Eight

The following morning, Candy sat at the kitchen table feeding Faith baby cereal. Between bites, while Faith pounded on the tray of her high chair, Candy's gaze flitted toward the living room. The Christmas stocking she'd knitted for Faith hung, sad and lopsided, from the mantel.

Candy sighed.

She'd been so proud of that stocking when she'd left Alice's yarn store. She'd come straight home with a bag of newly purchased knitting needles and three balls of yarn and gotten started on another one. And now, after sleeping on it—after *gifting* stocking number two to Dan as if it looked like one of the gorgeous hand-crafted items available for sale at the Christmas festival—Candy could see how truly pathetic it looked.

She gave Faith another spoonful of baby cereal and then shoveled a bite into her own mouth. *Pathetic.* Not the cereal—shockingly, it wasn't that bad—but her newbie attempt at knitting. How had she managed to chalk up another Christmas fail? If Candy had used one of those stockings as a set prop, Gabe would probably fire her.

Again.

"I'm terrible at this, aren't I?" she asked Faith in a singsong voice that Candy hoped might disguise her existential holiday crisis.

Faith squealed and kicked her little feet, currently clad in a pair of crocheted baby booties designed to look like Santa boots. Candy had managed to nail Christmas baby fashion, thanks to Melanie's boutique on Main Street. Her credit card was probably screaming in protest, but at least she'd gotten something right. Of course, she'd *still* yet to properly document Faith's first Christmas with a photo of her wearing said booties while snuggled adorably in Santa Claus's lap. She'd wanted to get the picture earlier, but she'd been distracted by last minute shopping and discouraged by yet another line in front of Santa's throne. There was still time, though.

Not much *time.* Candy glanced down at the clunky orthopedic boot on her foot. Dragging that thing around was putting a definite damper on her holiday to-do list. How was she supposed to strap Faith into a BabyBjörn and go snowshoeing in the Vermont woods with a sprained ankle?

Candy sighed. Snowshoeing was off the table. Maybe she should just haul herself back to the gazebo and sit there for the rest of her "break." She might have considered it, except the idea of sitting there with Faith all alone seemed even more depressing than limping around town in a Santa hat. There was only one thing to do. Press on.

Except before Candy could get up, clean the kitchen and head out to build a snowman, discover the recipe for the world's best hot cocoa or do something equally festive, she found herself reaching for her cell phone. Faith blinked her big blue eyes and smeared cereal on her high chair tray while Candy tapped the entry for Gabe's contact information.

Guilt tugged at her heart. She was in Lovestruck, the Christmas capital of Vermont, and she couldn't manage to forget about work long enough to say "Kris Kringle"? What sort of mother was she?

The kind that had just gotten rolled to voice mail, apparently. Gabe's outgoing message droned from her phone, followed by a beep. Candy tried not to read into it. Gabe was probably already in the studio, swamped with edits. Never mind the fact that it wasn't even eight in the morning yet in California.

She left a chirpy message, telling Gabe she was just checking in and letting him know that she'd sent an email with her Lovestruck address in case he wanted to FedEx her a script for the upcoming film they'd be working on in January. Totally normal behavior. Why would she possibly want to just relax and enjoy her forced break?

Candy ended the message and shoved her cell phone out of reach before she caved and called someone else. Surely she wasn't depressed enough to actually dial Brian.

Faith giggled and slapped her tiny palms on

the tray again. Candy envied her joy in the simplest of moments. Maybe the stocking wasn't such an epic fail, after all. Faith probably didn't care that it was all wonky and uneven.

Dan, on the other hand…

He'd probably tossed his straight in the trash. Candy might not blame him if he did. Whether he actually hung on to it or not, there was zero chance the stocking was hanging from his mantel.

"Come on, sweetheart." Candy stood, wiped Faith's hands and mouth clean and lifted her out of her high chair. She snuggled into Candy's arms, all softness and fresh baby powder scent. "We can't snowshoe, but there are other things we can do. *Important* things."

Candy glanced at her surroundings. She'd managed to spruce up her side of the duplex, but it was still missing the most important holiday decoration of all. That needed fixing. Today.

Half an hour later, bundled in up in her Burberry trench with Faith strapped to her chest in the BabyBjörn, Candy headed outside. It was snowing again—small flurries that seemed to float toward the ground in slow motion.

"We can do this," she said as she turned to

lock the door behind her. "It's not a blizzard, just a little dusting."

Candy wasn't entirely sure whom she was trying to convince, Faith or herself, since she'd technically never driven in snow before. It couldn't be that hard, could it?

She squared her shoulders, turned back around and plowed straight into Dan Manning's impressive chest.

"Where do you think you're going?" he said, catching her by the shoulders before she knocked him over. Not likely, considering he seemed as solid as a brick wall. "And why on earth do you think you need that thing?"

He glowered in the direction of the handsaw she was holding and then fixed his gaze with hers as he pried it from her grip.

Nice to see you, too, Scrooge McDoc.

"Hey, I need that." She reached for the saw, but he took a backward step and hid it behind his back like they were playing a game of keep-away on a school playground.

"No, you don't." He shook his offensively good-looking head. "You've got a sprained ankle, and there's a baby strapped to your chest. You definitely don't need to be carrying a weapon."

"It's a handsaw, the smallest one the hardware store carries. And in case you didn't notice, there's a blade guard on it." Did he truly think she would walk around with an exposed blade in one hand and a baby in the other? "It's hardly a weapon. If you must know, I'm going to use it to cut down a Christmas tree at the tree farm between here and Burlington."

"With this?" Dan held up the saw and let out a snort of laughter. "Impossible. You'd have better luck trying to karate chop a tree down."

"You just called it a dangerous weapon, and now it's too flimsy to chop down a tiny little Christmas tree?" Candy raised her eyebrows in challenge. There was definitely a flaw in his mansplainer logic. "Which one is it?"

The laughter in his eyes died. "You're injured. The last thing you should be doing is stomping through the woods trying to chop down a tree with this glorified nail file...or an ax or any other variety of sharp object." He narrowed his gaze at her Burberry trench. "And that coat definitely isn't warm enough for a Vermont forest."

"Forest? I thought it was a Christmas tree farm. That's what the website said. I imagined neat little rows of trees just off the side of the road."

He rolled his eyes. "Don't believe everything you see on television. This is Vermont, not a movie set. Trees grow in a forest, even when they grow in 'neat little rows.' And outside of town, where the salt trucks and snowplows don't make as many rounds, the roads are covered in snow. Are you prepared for that, too?"

Ugh, he was right, darn it. Right about everything. A chill had already permeated her designer coat, and she'd never considered that there might be more snow on the outskirts of town. Also, she didn't know the first thing about chopping down a tree. It had just seemed like such a charming idea when she'd jotted it down on her list of Christmas goals.

Where was a stuntman when she really and truly needed one?

"Stay here. I'll be right back," Dan said, and then he carried Candy's "glorified nail file" into his house and shut the door.

Unbelievable. He'd hijacked her saw. If he wasn't careful, she was going to end up leaving him a terrible review on Airbnb. Had he actually taken care of her after her spill at the skating pond, or had she merely hallucinated that random act of kindness?

"What just happened, Faith?" Candy muttered.

Faith's only response was a merry little giggle.

Before Candy could explain how nonhilarious the situation was, Dan's door flew open and he walked back out onto the porch. Her saw was nowhere to be seen. He carried a huge bright orange puffer coat in his hand instead.

"Take off that windbreaker," he said, shooting one of his disapproving glares at the trench that had cost her almost a full month's salary.

"This isn't a windbreaker. It's *Burberry*." Candy lifted her chin, but when her teeth started chattering, she did as he said.

Dan helped her out of it and then slid the puffer coat onto her arms while Faith squealed her approval.

The coat smelled like pine and frost, with a hint of maple. The sleeves extended past her fingertips. Clearly, it had come from Dan's personal wardrobe.

"Better, isn't it?" His gaze met hers, and suddenly, her teeth stopped chattering. Warmth spread through her, from the tips of her covered fingers all the way down to her toes.

"For your information, I'd intended to get a new coat. I just haven't had time," Candy said, but her words had lost their bite.

His lips curved into a crooked smile. *Finally.* "Happy to save you a shopping trip."

It was just as well. Candy wouldn't have even known where to get a coat like the one he'd just draped over her. Something told her there wasn't a boutique that sold Vermont-approved puffer coats within a hundred miles of LA.

"My saw?" she prompted.

But he just walked past her, shaking his head. "You don't need that thing. I've got a proper ax in the car."

"But…"

He opened the passenger-side door of his SUV and pointed inside. "Get in. I'll get Faith's car seat out of your vehicle. I'm going with you."

Candy blinked.

Be careful what you wish for.

It looked like she'd just found her stuntman.

Less than two hours later, Dan tightened the bungee cord that held a five-foot blue spruce to the top of his SUV while Candy snapped his picture…again.

From the minute they'd stepped out of the car at the Sugar Frost Family Christmas Tree Farm, she'd been camera-happy. She snapped numerous pictures of the farm itself and its rows of trees, which she'd gushed about being perfectly spaced "like little toy soldiers." When a passerby had offered to take a photo of the three of them—Dan, Candy and Faith—in front of the tree she'd chosen, Candy had gone positively ecstatic. Dan had really had no choice but to acquiesce. Afterward, at Candy's insistence, he'd then posed for numerous "action shots" while doing the chopping.

"Just how much memory do you have on that iPhone?" he asked, giving the bungee a final tug.

Snow crunched under his feet as he hopped down from the running board and started tugging off his utility gloves.

"You look ridiculously manly. I'm loving this lumberjack aesthetic you've got going on right now. You could be on a Christmas card…or a paper towel commercial. I could get you cast in an instant." The shutter on Candy's phone clicked again. "And I've got loads of memory on my phone. Why do you ask?"

Dan stepped closer, until he could feel her

breath warming his face. The grin on Candy's mouth faded as he wrapped his fingertips around her cell and wrestled it from her grasp.

"Hey." She pouted, and it took superhuman resistance not to let his gaze drop to her plush bottom lip.

Yes, Candy Cane's off-the-charts enthusiasm for the holidays was every bit as grating in the wilderness as it was within the Lovestruck town limits, but out here, it was also sort of... charming.

Candy, her ugly Christmas sweater (how many of those did the woman actually own?) and Faith's bright red snowsuit, scattered with romping cartoon reindeer, fit right in with the unexpected wave of nostalgia that had washed over Dan when the Christmas tree farm had come into view. He'd visited this same farm with his parents for years as a kid. Being here again, Dan felt like he'd been dropped into a snow globe that someone had given a good hard shake, and shockingly...he didn't altogether hate it. Which, in and of itself, should have been alarming. But try as he might, Dan found it difficult to fight off the impending threat of Christmas cheer, consumed as he was with his unofficial audition to become the next Bounty paper towel guy.

"Enough with the pictures." He slid Candy's phone into his coat pocket. "If this was a Christmas movie, wouldn't my character be giving yours a lecture about living in the moment? Isn't that the sort of lesson those films try to impart?"

Her lips quirked into a half grin. And yes, Dan let his gaze linger on that red-ribbon smile of hers a beat too long. He was only human, after all.

"Oh my gosh, are you giving me a lecture about living in the moment?" She jabbed her pointer finger at his chest. "You—the man without a single decoration in his home—want to make sure I soak up the ambience of this Christmas tree farm without the added distraction of modern technology?"

Faith babbled in her BabyBjörn and Candy rested a hand on the infant's tiny chest. Dan gave one of Faith's feet an affectionate squeeze.

"I guess I do, yeah." He shrugged. "Although I suppose my lecture came too late since we're finished."

"What? No, we're not." Candy tilted her head, and alarm bells started going off in Dan's mind.

He waved toward the blue spruce strapped to the roof of his car. "Um, yes we are."

He'd been shocked at how quickly she'd chosen a tree. Candy definitely seemed like the type to examine every Douglas fir, Scotch pine and blue spruce on the farm before making a selection. He should've known something was amiss.

Candy spun on her heel and started marching back toward the rows of trees. "The art director on all of our Christmas films has a strict rule. Do you want to know what it is?"

Dan grabbed his ax and followed. *What now?* "I might, but I'm afraid to ask."

"The rule states that we've got to have a Christmas tree in every shot. It's a trick to make sure every frame of the film looks festive."

That seemed liked overkill to Dan, but what did he care? They weren't in a movie, no matter how much it sometimes felt that way in Candy's presence. "And what does this rule have to do with the here and now?"

"It's easily translatable to the real world." She shrugged one shoulder as she stopped in front of a tiny fir tree. "A tree in every frame becomes a tree in every room of the house. Doesn't that sound lovely?"

It didn't sound lovely. It sounded completely bonkers.

"No." Dan snorted. "Hard pass." He would've tossed his ax on the ground if he hadn't been concerned she might pick it up and start whacking away at the sapling on her own.

"They don't have to be huge," she countered.

"So just a small live tree in *every single room* of my house that you've rented for the holiday? Sounds completely reasonable and not at all over-the-top."

She waved a hand at the sapling. "Are you going to cut it down or shall I try the karate-chop technique you mentioned?"

"You're serious. You actually want a Christmas tree for every room." Dan did the math in his head. The duplex was small, but counting the bathroom, they were talking about six trees. *Six.* "I'm not sure we can fit six trees on top of my car, no matter how small they are."

She laughed. "Don't be silly. We're not getting six trees."

Dan had never been so happy to have misinterpreted a conversation in his life. "Good. For a minute there—"

"We're getting seven." Candy held up seven

fingers. Faith grabbed onto one of them with a tiny fist.

Why, oh why, had he insisted on accompanying them on this mission? Oh right, he'd wanted to avoid having to treat Candy for frostbite in addition to her sprained ankle...not to mention the tetanus shot he would have been forced to give her if she'd cut herself with her sad little saw.

"Why seven?" he asked, even though every thought in his head was screaming at him to stop asking questions and getting himself even more entrenched in Candy's Christmas madness. "Your side of the duplex only has six rooms."

"The seventh one is for your side." She flashed him a smile.

His jaw automatically clenched. "Candy."

"Come on. Just one little tree. It can be tabletop size if you want." She threw her arms open wide.

One of her hands banged into a tree branch, dislodging a pile of snow from an upper bough. A shower of white rained down over the three of them, their own private snowstorm. Faith's big blue eyes went as wide as saucers.

"This is all for her, you know. Lovestruck,

the pictures, the trees, all of it," Candy said, grinning down at the baby.

Something inside Dan loosened and un-spooled like a ribbon. "The pictures you've been taking all afternoon are for Faith?"

"Yes. This is her first Christmas, and I'm so new to all of this. I want to make it happy for her. I want to capture every moment so when she's older I can tell her all about her very first holiday. About Lovestruck. About the trees in every room…" Her eyes softened and the look she gave him nearly brought him to his knees. "About you."

They stood there for a moment with only the trees as their witnesses. Pine needles stirred gently in the winter wind as Dan took a deep inhale of evergreen-scented air and reached to brush a snowflake from Candy's mouth. She inhaled sharply when the pad of his thumb brushed against the impossible softness of her bottom lip.

"So what you're saying is that I'm not actu-ally going to be cast in a paper towel commer-cial," he murmured as he let his fingertips move to cup her cheek.

"Disappointed?" she whispered.

When it came to Candy? Never. It was impossible to feel anything but optimistic and hopeful in her presence…

…whether he wanted to or not.

Dan had just never realized how much he wanted to feel that way, until she'd breezed into his life with her ugly Christmas sweaters, her twelve-foot reindeer and her unflinching earnestness. And now… He *wanted*. Oh, how he wanted.

He wanted to give in and let her put a sad Charlie Brown tabletop Christmas tree right in the center of his living room. He wanted to pose for more goofy pictures for her to save for Faith. Heaven help him, he wanted *her*.

Candy.

It would never work. How could it? They didn't have a thing in common—not even geographically—and Dan wasn't in the habit of having meaningless flings. Even if he had been, he was fully aware that there wasn't a thing about Candy that could ever be described as meaningless. While he'd been doing his best to coast through December in neutral, she'd been attacking each moment with purpose and intention. She and Faith deserved better than the likes of him, especially at Christmas.

Ever so slowly, Dan removed his hand from

Candy's face and pretended not to notice the flash of disappointment in her gaze.

"Disappointed?" He gave her a smile, frozen in place by the crisp, Vermont air and years of holiday practice. "Not a bit."

Chapter Nine

"You've got to be kidding me. You have six Christmas trees?" Madison stared at Candy, wide-eyed over the top of a martini glass full of a ruby-red concoction that the firemen at Cap McBride's holiday party were calling "jingle juice."

Felicity blinked. "Six…as in half a dozen?"

Candy sipped her own glass of jingle juice and nodded. "One for every room. It's…kind of a film thing."

She didn't want to explain. It had seemed like such a fun idea back at the Christmas tree farm, and miraculously, Dan had indulged her. He'd gamely chopped down a tree for each room of the duplex, plus a tiny one for his home as well. The SUV had looked like a mini-forest on wheels as they'd driven back to the duplex.

Even stranger, they'd had a moment out there among the evergreens. For a second, Candy had actually thought Dan wanted to kiss her. His fingertips had been so warm and tender when he'd touched her face. Every part of her had wanted to lean into him, like the trees surrounding them all stretched toward the sun. He'd seemed as light and open as a clear blue sky, and then...

Then, something had changed. His eyes had gone as dark as quickly as a strand of Christmas lights that had just been unplugged. Candy couldn't figure out what had changed, but something definitely had. The easy camaraderie between them just—*poof*—vanished.

When they got back to Lovestruck, he'd laid down the law about putting lights on the trees. Only one strand per tree, to avoid overloading the electrical sockets. Candy assured him that she could live with that. If he'd been willing to go along with her nutty plan to have a tree in every room, the least she could do was to agree to his rule about lights.

But the magic of the afternoon had been well and truly over. When she'd invited him to stay and make popcorn garland, he'd made some sort of excuse about getting to bed early. Candy had heard the television droning on the other side of the wall for the entire night, all the way up until the moment she'd crawled into bed. For all she knew, his sweet little tree was still sitting in his home, completely unadorned— no popcorn garland, no lights, no ornaments. Bah humbug.

"A tree in every room. That sounds wonderful." Madison sighed. "Except for the part where I'd have to keep twin toddlers from undecorating them between now and Christmas."

"I guess I might have to reevaluate things when Faith becomes more mobile," Candy said with a laugh. Although, who knew where she'd be at that point. Most holidays, she was busy working on a film. Once her professional life got back on track, she probably wouldn't have time for things like Christmas tree farms and popcorn garland.

This holiday was one of a kind. Special.

At least that was the plan… Gabe had yet to return Candy's call, despite the fact that she'd followed it up with a few text messages. She was beginning to wonder if her firing might not be altogether temporary.

Candy wasn't going to worry about her job right now, though—not when she was supposed to be enjoying a holiday party in a small-town fire station. This was the stuff Christmas movie aesthetics were made of.

She leaned closer to Felicity and Melanie. "Are you both sure that I'm actually allowed to be here? Isn't this supposed to be a special party for first responders?"

Not that she was complaining.

Alice and her knitting klatch were on group babysitting duty, and this was the first adult evening Candy had experienced since Faith had come to live with her. She'd been teetering between ecstatic and terrified since she'd walked through the big red doors of the firehouse's apparatus bay. She wasn't sure she knew what to do without a baby on her hip anymore.

"Madison invited you. Of course you're supposed to be here. She and Cap are hosting this shindig. It's for the first responders, plus a few special guests," Felicity said.

Melanie winked. "That makes you special, Candy. Felicity and I are just our husbands' plus-ones."

Candy glanced around the firehouse, dripping with twinkle lights, swags of evergreen and red velvet bows. A tall Christmas tree topped with a fire helmet stood in the corner of the station's common area. Makeshift fire hose garland was wrapped around the Douglas fir, and the tree skirt was fashioned from the bulky jacket of a firefighter's turnout gear. Beyond the station's opened garage doors, snow swirled against the dark winter sky. It was so perfect and atmospheric that if Candy hadn't known better, she would have thought Gabe's set designer had stopped by Lovestruck and done a little decorating.

"I definitely *feel* special," she said as Felicity's husband, Wade, traded her empty martini glass for a full one. "And I promise that's not just the jingle juice talking."

Wade wrapped an arm around Felicity and they all clinked glasses.

But Candy's cocktail paused halfway to her mouth when she spotted Dan walking through the firehouse door.

She blinked. Hard.

"What's he doing here?" she blurted. Then she set her drink down on a nearby table. Perhaps one glass of jingle juice was her limit.

"Who?" Wade followed her gaze. When he spied Dan chatting with Cap near the entryway, he turned back toward Candy and grinned. "You mean Dr. Dan?"

"That's definitely who she means," Felicity said with a smirk.

Candy shook her head. "I didn't mean anything by it. Honestly. He's my…" She suddenly had no clue how to complete that sentence. Stuntman? Doctor? Friend? "…landlord."

It was the truth, but as they said in television legal dramas, it wasn't the *whole* truth.

Yes, Dan was her landlord. He was all those other things, too. But despite his nonsensical aversion to popcorn garland—or most forms of holiday fun, in general—he'd also started to feel like something more.

It didn't make a bit of sense, but Candy couldn't deny it. Just the sight of him across the room was making her heart pound in a way that it never did in the presence of a *real* stuntperson.

She took a gulp of air and snatched her glass back up off the table. Red liquid sloshed over the rim. *Jingle all the way.*

"It's just that he's not all that into Christmas. I'm a little surprised to see him at a holiday party," she said, reminding herself that there was nothing attractive about a man who hated holiday lawn ornaments. Come to think of it, he really needed to stop wearing those cute Christmas ties. It was false advertising to the highest order.

Wade paused and seemed to consider her comment. "I guess I never realized he wasn't into Christmas. We invite him to pretty much all the department functions. He's practically an honorary firefighter."

"He volunteers for the first aid station at the Christmas festival so the firefighters and EMS team can take the time off," Madison said.

Felicity nodded. "He helps out with the boot drive fundraiser, too. He spends as much time standing on Main Street trying to drum up donations as the firefighters do."

Wade held up a finger. "More importantly, he's joined the Fancy patrol."

"The Fancy patrol? What on earth is that?" Candy's gaze flicked toward Madison and Felicity, but they just nodded in agreement.

"Fancy is a cat whose mission the past few years has been to terrorize the LFD," Felicity said after a beat.

Candy laughed...until she realized no one

else had cracked a smile. "Wait, you're serious? Is she a mountain lion or a puma or something?"

Or were mountain lions and pumas the same thing? Candy wasn't sure. Dangerous wild cats didn't roam free in LA the way that camels and donkeys took to the streets in Lovestruck.

"Worse. She's a Persian," Wade said, dead serious.

Candy bit back a smile. "Aren't Persians cute little fluff ball house cats? The ones that look like kittens even after they grow up?"

"Not this one." Wade snorted. "She's cute, physically, but she uses her adorableness like a weapon."

"Fancy once put Jack in the hospital," Madison said.

Candy was at a loss. "I can't believe what I'm hearing, you guys."

"Believe it. She climbs trees and hangs out up there until we're forced to go get her." Wade held up a hand like a claw and made a *rawrr* sound. "That's when she attacks."

"I'm trying really hard not to laugh right now, I swear." Candy crossed her heart. "But the fact that this fire station rescues kittens in trees is beyond sweet. I have to smile. I can't help it."

She couldn't imagine her big-city fire department doing such a thing. Come to think of it, she couldn't imagine them throwing a holiday party in the firehouse either. In Lovestruck, the firehouse seemed like the backbone of the community. Main Street, as modest as it was, truly seemed like the glue that held the town together, just like all those fictional sweet places she'd created for TV.

Except Lovestruck was real, and so were the people who lived here. It made Candy wonder why anyone would ever want to leave.

She frowned into her drink. *Except me. I can't wait to get my life back.* The thought was automatic, reflexive. Her work was usually her vacation, her escape from cold reality.

Now the strange feeling of wistfulness that came over her sent a different message. This reality was as good as an escape. Maybe even better. Leaving Lovestruck was going to be hard, and she wasn't even sure why. She should be used to this sort of thing. Being on holiday was like shooting on location. After a few weeks, things wrapped up and people moved on. Period. Her time in Lovestruck shouldn't be any different.

Except it was. Leaving already felt different, and she hadn't even said goodbye yet. She wasn't playing make-believe here.

"Well, we do save kittens, and now the town pediatrician goes with us every time Fancy gets in trouble." Wade shrugged. "It started when Cap jokingly asked him if he could prescribe the cat some Valium. I guess Dr. Dan wanted to see Fancy in action, so he came along on the next call. He climbed up the fire truck ladder like a pro. I don't know what he said or did to that cat, but it worked. Fancy is a marshmallow whenever Dan's around."

Candy glanced at Dan, still talking to Cap over by the fire-themed Christmas tree. And she realized that she'd never felt such an affinity with a kitten before.

"You should have seen him up in that tree, sweet-talking the cat." Wade narrowed his gaze at Candy. "Dr. Dan's a great guy. Are you sure he doesn't like Christmas?"

"Um…"

He didn't like Christmas. That was a fact— at least she thought it was—but Candy wasn't so sure of anything anymore.

And when Dan's gaze locked with hers across the crowded room, she had the sudden urge to climb a tree and hide, Fancy-style. Unfortunately, there wasn't one of Lovestruck's famous sugar maple trees in sight. Even if there had been, Dr. Dan probably would have followed her up there, charmed the socks off her and then disappeared.

Just like he always did.

"I'm sure he loves Christmas," she lied. Anything to get out of this uncomfortable conversation. "Doesn't everyone?"

Then she excused herself to go outside and get some air, away from the mistletoe and merriment.

Like a scaredy-cat.

"Here you are." Dan stepped out onto the back deck of the firehouse where Candy stood with her arms wrapped around herself, face tipped upward so that snow flurries danced against her skin.

His head told him to give her another lecture about wearing proper outerwear in Vermont. She had to be freezing. But his body had other ideas—ideas that involved sliding his hand onto the small of her back, pulling her close and whispering something into her ear that would hopefully make her feel warm all over.

He cleared his throat and shoved his hands in his pockets to stop himself from acting on the nonsensical impulse. "I knew I saw you earlier, but I was beginning to think it was just a dream."

She swiveled her gaze toward him, dark lashes tipped with snow. "A Scrooge-style dream? Who did you think I was—Christmas past, present or future?"

Dan's heart balled into a fist in his chest. *All three, sweetheart.* She looked like a snow queen out here in the darkness, the beginning, the middle and the end of a place he hadn't allowed himself to visit in years.

He tilted his head to better study her warm brown eyes. Either he was imagining things, or she seemed uncharacteristically melancholy. "Which Christmas do you want to be?"

"Christmas past," she said automatically. Her cheeks filled with color—holly berry red, visible even in the starlight. "I suppose."

Same. He wanted to ask her to elaborate, but was worried she might reciprocate. So instead he smiled and said, "It looks like your ankle is feeling better."

She glanced down at her feet. Instead of her air cast, she was wearing lush red heels with delicate rhinestone ankle straps. "Much. It's still a tiny bit sore, but this is a party. I wanted to dress up."

"Well, you look…" He blew out a breath. She looked like a Christmas dream come true, an angel in red satin. "…beautiful."

The smile that came to her lips nearly knocked him off his feet.

He cleared his throat. "I suppose I shouldn't be surprised to see you here. I've lived here for over a decade and you might know more people in Lovestruck than I do. You have an uncanny knack for making friends."

"Says the only man in Vermont capable of taming Fancy the Persian." She arched an eyebrow. "Or so I hear."

"Someone told you about that? Don't tell me it was Frances." It was hopeless. The woman didn't know the meaning of the word *boundaries* and never would.

"It was Wade, actually. And don't worry—he had nothing but wonderful things to say about you. In fact, he didn't believe me when I told him you don't like Christmas."

"Surely you didn't get a babysitter and get all

dressed up to come to this party and hear about my way with kittens." He laughed, an attempt at levity, but he may as well have said that he hadn't been able to take his eyes off her since she'd walked through the door.

Probably because he hadn't.

She'd traded her adorably dorky ugly Christmas sweaters and faded jeans for a retro party dress with a fitted bodice and a tulle skirt that floated around her legs like a cherry pie ballerina dream. He liked knowing that there was another side to Candy than the one he'd already seen. Of course there was, just like there were parts of him that she knew nothing about.

And never will.

"Why don't you?" she asked, undeterred. "Like Christmas, I mean. You're clearly a good person. I might even like you, despite my every effort not to. So, please. Spill the beans. What could a charming, kitten-saving small-town doctor who spends his free time doing volunteer work for the fire department possibly have against Christmas?"

She'd said the words with a hint of flirtation in her voice, but they still felt like a blow to the chest.

Dan took a backward step. He shook his head

and let out a breath that hung suspended between them in the air. "Candy. I—"

He couldn't do this. Not here. Not now.

"Never mind. I shouldn't have asked." The smile she gave him was an arrow to his heart, the saddest thing he'd ever seen. She looked down at her stilettos, red as a Valentine against the snow. "It's clearly none of my business. I'm just a stranger. Once Christmas is over, we'll never even see each other and—"

"Don't say that," Dan said quietly. His voice was scarcely more than a whisper, but the night was so quiet, so tender that it seemed shockingly loud.

Candy glanced up. "But—"

"I don't want us to be strangers," Dan said. He wasn't sure why the notion upset him so much. He just knew that the idea sounded wholly unacceptable.

"Okay." She took a deep breath. "I'll go first, then. Maybe if I tell you something deeply personal about myself, you'll eventually do the same."

He shook his head and started to tell her that wasn't how this was going to work. Dan never talked about his feelings about Christmas— with anyone—and he wasn't going to start now. It was just another day on the calendar. He shouldn't have to explain himself.

But before he could utter a word, Candy lifted her chin and said the very last words he'd expected to hear.

"The gazebo brought me back here."

Dan went still. He had to force his next words out. "I don't understand. The gazebo?"

"The one in the town square." She waved a hand in the direction of the snow-laden boughs of the Lovestruck Christmas tree, spread above Main Street like angel wings. From where they stood, Dan could just make out the lights of the gazebo, glittering behind the great tree like a golden promise. "Where we met for the first time."

"Where we met," he echoed as a chill coursed through him. The temperature was dropping by the minute and a snowstorm was due any day. They needed to go back inside, but he couldn't seem to move a muscle.

"It's where I had my first kiss." She lit up at the memory of it. Positively glowed. "Years ago, on Christmas Eve. I was just a teenager, visiting Lovestruck with my family, and I met a boy who gave me the most magical moment of my life. Weeks after that Christmas, everything sort of fell apart. I lost my parents and I lost my hope. I've been trying to get it back ever since."

She swallowed, and Dan traced the movement up and down the slender column of her throat. When he met her eyes again, they were filled with unshed tears.

"So there you have it. My deepest, darkest secret. I don't know what I'm doing anymore—with Faith, with my career. Not even when it comes to Christmas. I came back to Lovestruck, back to that gazebo, trying to find magic and…"

"And instead you found me," he said, and the ache in his tone was like a heartbreak, even to his own ears.

She looked at him, eyes and heart open wide, and he just knew she expected him to reciprocate. But he couldn't…especially not after the revelation she'd just shared.

Then her gaze dropped to his mouth, and he realized he was wrong. She didn't want words from him. She wanted something else— something more intimate that he was powerless to resist. So when she rose up on tiptoe, wrapped her arms around his neck and brushed her lips against his, Dan didn't hesitate.

He kissed her back as if his life depended on it, as if she could breathe hope into his soul with the heat of her candy-sweet mouth and he could do the same for her.

He kissed her as if the whimsical, winsome Candy Cane was Christmas itself.

Chapter Ten

What was she doing? What were *they* doing?
Kissing Dan Manning wasn't part of the plan.
Candy wasn't supposed to be doing this. She
wasn't supposed to be kissing *anyone*, least of
all her cranky neighbor. Her life was confusing
enough as it was at the moment. Her career might
be hanging by a thread and she still had no idea
how to balance her demanding work schedule
with taking care of Faith. She definitely didn't
need to add anything to the mix as topsy-turvy
as developing feelings for someone…not even
someone who just might not be as Grinchy as

he'd let her believe. At least not during January through November, apparently.

But his mouth was so warm and the way he cupped her face as his lips moved against hers was so gentle, so tender that she felt precious and rare, like a vintage mercury glass ornament.

Timeless.

It's just a kiss, she told herself. *It doesn't have to mean anything.*

But the sound of her racing pulse drowned out her inner voice, right along with everything else. Her thoughts were a whirl. All she could do was feel—Dan's fingertips as they moved from her face to her hair, the softness of his cashmere coat beneath her hands, the wild beat of his heart against hers. Whom was she trying to fool? This was no ordinary kiss. It was…

Magic. Just like that Christmas Eve so long ago at the gazebo.

"Hey, you two. I—" Wade's voice stuttered to a halt as he walked out onto the deck. He glanced back and forth between Candy and Dan and held up his hands. "So sorry. I didn't mean to interrupt."

A groan escaped Dan just as Candy took a big, backward leap away from him. She didn't even know why she did it. The action was pure instinct, as if they were teenagers who'd just been caught making out in the hall at school.

"Mistletoe," she blurted.

Wade bit back a smile.

Dan looked above their heads and frowned. There wasn't a sprig of mistletoe in sight.

"It was there a second ago," she said.

Why was she still talking? What difference did it make if Wade—or the entire Lovestruck Fire Department, for that matter—thought she went around kissing random men at holiday parties?

Not that Dan was some random man. She was beginning to think he just might be the opposite… an *exceptional* man. And the prospect scared the life out of her.

"You're probably right." Dan arched an eyebrow. She couldn't tell if he was amused or furious. "I'm certain I saw a whole bushel of mistletoe up there earlier."

A bushel? Really? Couldn't he have backed her up in any sort of sensible way?

"Vanishing mistletoe aside, I thought you might want to come in. We're about to do the Christmas ornament relay." Wade winked. "Or not. If you'd rather stay out here…"

"Nope." Candy drew herself up and pasted on a smile. "An ornament relay sounds fabulous. We're in."

She grabbed Dan's arm and dragged him back inside the firehouse. Wade followed, laughing behind them, merry as could be.

Full disclosure: Candy had no idea what an ornament relay even was. But if participating in one got the attention off her and Dan's impromptu Christmas kiss, she was all for it.

No sooner had they joined the rest of the party in the apparatus bay, though, than Dan's expression slammed closed like a book.

"What's wrong?" she murmured after Felicity handed her a spoon and declared that she and Dan would be partners. *Subtle, Felicity. Real subtle.*

Dan eyed the spoon and held up his hands. "I don't do Christmas party games."

"Who are you? Rudolph?" She rolled her eyes. "You know he really *wanted* to play reindeer games, right? He was super sad that he was never invited."

Dan didn't crack a smile.

Felicity stood in the center of the room, explaining the rules of the game. "Okay, everyone. This is just like the traditional egg relay everyone played in elementary school. One member of your team is going to line up against the far wall and your other half is going to be on the opposite side, facing you."

Candy glanced up at Dan, wondering if his thoughts had snagged on the words *other half*, like hers had. But the set of his jaw was as hard as granite and his expression as blank as it always was whenever he was within five feet of a string of Christmas garland.

Felicity continued. "I'm going to place a glass ornament on everyone's spoons and you're going to run to your partner as fast as you can without dropping it, pass them the spoon and then they're going to carry it to the Christmas tree." She waved toward the big evergreen situated between the two red fire engines with a Vanna White–style flourish. "The first team to get their spoon and unbroken ornament to the tree wins!"

They were going to *crush* this. Candy had dominated the egg relay at track and field day in elementary school. She and her partner had won every year, from first grade all the way through sixth.

She gripped her spoon and turned to beam

at Dan. "Why don't you go first? I can sprint our ornament to the finish."

Dan shook his head. "I said no."

"Wait." She blinked. "It's a relay race. You can't leave me without a partner."

Dan's gaze darted to a group of firefighters gathered around the punch bowl in the kitchen. "I'm sure you can find someone else."

"But…" Candy's face went hot.

Two seconds ago, they'd been kissing in the snow and now he'd rather pawn her off on somebody else than run across the room with an ornament on a spoon.

Dan sighed. "But what?"

But I don't want someone else. I want you.

"Here you go!" Felicity grinned as she stopped beside them just long enough to drop a glittery heart-shaped ornament into Candy's spoon. Then she winked at Candy and moved on.

Had everyone at the party already heard that Wade had caught them in an imaginary mistletoe moment?

Candy took a deep breath and met Dan's gaze. "Never mind. You're right. I'm sure one of the firemen over there would be delighted to be my partner."

She searched his face for a hint of jealousy. A muscle in his neck flexed, but he said nothing.

And suddenly, Candy was irrationally furious. She was starting to sweat beneath the bodice of her pretty Christmas dress. She'd just bared her soul to Dan. She just *kissed* him, and still he refused to budge an inch. What was his problem?

"Tell me." She threw up a hand, the other one shaking enough to rock the ornament in its spoon. Around them, the other partygoers started lining up for the relay. The air smelled like eggnog and roasted chestnuts. "Are you really not going to talk to me about why all of this seems to bother you so much?"

She wasn't being fair and she knew it. They were no longer in private. They were surrounded by people, ornaments and silver spoons as witnesses, but she couldn't seem to stop the words from tumbling out of her mouth.

"I think I'm going to go," Dan said quietly.

Of course he was.

Candy felt like crying. What was she even doing here? She barely knew these people. Why was she spending precious holiday time with people she'd never see again after Christmas?

Lovestruck wasn't any more real or permanent than a film set.

She should have stayed home with Faith and tried to check another item off her holiday to-do list. The gingerbread house she'd researched on the internet wasn't going to make itself.

"Don't go," she said, hating the way her voice cracked.

It was just a kiss. There's nothing to be embarrassed about. But she *was* embarrassed. Christmas kisses were supposed to be special—they were the climax of every movie she'd ever worked on. Each whimsical, romantic frame led up to the kiss. Never once had she considered that after the kiss was over, the two main characters would bicker over a spoon relay.

This is what she got for living in a holiday fantasy land three hundred sixty five days a year. Apparently, she'd forgotten how the real world worked.

"It's okay, really. I have an early morning tomorrow. You stay and have a good time." Dan gave the spoon in her hand a gentle tap, and his eyes softened, but the tenderness in his gaze was laced with a sadness that made Candy's heart ache. "This whole scene is right up your alley. I wouldn't want you to miss it."

Then he bent to brush his lips against her cheek, leaving her more confused than ever—so much so that she forgot all about the game and let her arms drop to her sides. Her little glass heart fell from the spoon and shattered against the concrete floor just as Dan's back disappeared from view.

The following morning started even earlier for Dan than he'd anticipated. His phone rang at five in the morning, a solid hour before he usually got up.

Not that it mattered, since he'd been awake half the night. As it turned out, guilt and insomnia went hand in hand. Maybe it hadn't been guilt so much as regret. Dan wasn't sure. All he knew was that he felt like a jerk for leaving Candy at the party.

He'd tried telling himself that it hadn't really mattered. They'd arrived separately, so there was no reason why he should have felt compelled to stay by her side for the duration of the evening. He hadn't even known she'd be there. But she'd kissed him…and that sweet, sublime touch of her lips had changed everything.

No, that wasn't quite true, was it? Things had

changed *before* she'd kissed him—mere seconds before. The kiss had simply sealed the deal.

"Okay, I'm going up," Dan said, trying his best to focus on the early-morning task at hand.

Climbing a ladder that extended from a fire truck to the frosty limbs of a sugar maple tree was an activity that required concentration—particularly when a fluffy cat was actively trying to push him back down. Dan knew this from experience.

"You sure you're okay with this?" Wade said as he offered Dan a fire helmet.

He took it and jammed it onto his head. "Fine. Why?"

"You just seem a little distracted this morning." Wade shrugged, and the bulk of his turnout coat rustled. "And I couldn't help noticing how early you left last night…"

"I said it's fine." Dan focused on pulling on a pair of work gloves so he wouldn't have to meet Wade's gaze. But he could feel the weight of Wade's stare, all the same.

"Look, man. I can't let you go up there if you're not in the right frame of mind." Wade pointed toward the tree, where Fancy was curled into a furry little ball, wailing as loud as the siren on the LFD's rig. "You could get hurt."

Dan arched an eyebrow. "Is this your way of forcing me to talk?"

"No pressure. Truly. I just want to make sure you're safe up there."

"So this line of questioning doesn't have anything to do with the fact that you found Candy and me kissing on the deck?"

"You're looking at me like I'm the kid who caught his mommy kissing Santa Claus." Wade snorted. "You and Candy are grown-ups. It's none of my business."

"Yet, here we are. Talking about it," Dan countered.

"You're the one who brought it up, my friend." Wade waggled his eyebrows. "So maybe deep down, you actually *want* to talk about it."

Busted.

Dan glanced up at the cat in the tree and back at his friend, trying to figure out which option would be less painful. He went with the more excruciating choice, nevertheless.

"How was she after I left last night?" he asked.

"She and her partner won the ornament relay." Wade shook his head. "By a lot. Your girl is competitive."

"She's not my girl," Dan said automatically.

"Something tells me she could be." Wade gave him a meaningful look. "If that's what you wanted."

It didn't matter what Dan wanted. Not in this case. "We're as opposite as night and day. Not to mention the fact that she lives across the country."

Above them, Fancy stared down with piercing ice-blue eyes, as if even the cat had opinions about Dan's love life. Or lack thereof.

"There's this new invention called airplanes. Maybe you've heard of them?" Wade reached to hold the ladder in place.

"It's not that simple," Dan said without elaborating.

How was he supposed to explain the crux of the problem? Candy had broken down and told him she didn't know what she was doing, but at least she was still trying. She was still doing her best to create the holiday magic she wanted so badly to experience…for real. Whereas he'd given up on the magic a long, long time ago.

Her belief in Christmas was pure—far too pure for him to even think about being a part of it. She felt a little bit lost, but she still had the most precious thing of all. Hope.

But Dan couldn't say any of those things to Wade without explaining the reasons why he wasn't the one to help Candy find her way. How could he? He wasn't simply lost. He'd turned his back on the holidays and willingly walked away, and now he was so far gone that he couldn't have found his way back if he tried.

He swallowed hard and did his best not to think about the gazebo, shining in the dark, pulling him back. Pulling him *home*.

"Like I said, it's your business. But if you ever want to talk, I'm here," Wade said.

Fancy let out a mournful meow and when both men looked up at the cat, she swiped at the air with a paw, claws extended.

Dan winced. "I'd better get up there. She's getting more upset by the minute."

"Better you than me," Wade muttered, and then his gaze flitted toward the sky beyond the snowy boughs of the sugar maple. "Fancy isn't the only thing looking angry today. Get a load of those clouds."

Dan took a closer look at his surroundings. The sky was pearly gray, filled with an angry row of thunderheads that seemed almost low enough to reach out and touch. Wade was right. He really needed to get his head in the game.

"We're expecting more snow the next few days, aren't we?" He placed a foot on the ladder's lowest rung to test its stability.

Wade nodded. "Yep. A lot of it, from the looks of things."

"I'm going up and getting that cat before the sky breaks open," Dan said.

A storm was on its way. He would have known, even if the evidence hadn't been written in the clouds. He'd felt it in his bones since the moment he'd stepped out into the snowy darkness with Candy.

In some ways, he was still out there with his hands in her hair, lips moving against hers, hearts crashing against one another in the frosty night. It had been sweeter than peppermint candy, and he hadn't wanted it to end. But that was the way with Christmas, wasn't it? Even when you embraced it, it only lasted a season…a day.

Whether it ended with a tender kiss or went up in flames, it ended all the same.

Chapter Eleven

Candy spent the day after the fire department Christmas party gluing together chunks of gingerbread with icing in an attempt to construct a gingerbread house. Like every other holiday craft she'd attempted, the end result was a hot mess.

By the time evening rolled around, all she had to show for her efforts was a pile of gingerbread rubble dotted with colorful gumdrops and globs of icing that dripped from the platter onto the kitchen counter. Faith had enjoyed herself, though. She'd smeared icing all over the tray of her high chair with glee, and the house was rich with the scents of nutmeg and spice.

Better yet, the ramshackle gingerbread house had kept Candy so occupied that she only thought about kissing Dan a handful of times. One or two hundred, tops.

It had been a silly, stupid moment of weakness—one that wouldn't be repeated, even if real, actual mistletoe sprang up out of nowhere and started hanging from every square inch of the ceiling. Because clearly it had been a mistake and she'd somehow misread the warmth between her and Dan for something it wasn't. If he'd really wanted to kiss her, he wouldn't have left the party immediately afterward.

But it was fine. Truly. She knew where she stood now. She and Dan were neighbors, and nothing more. She needed to stop buying him wreaths, knitting him stockings and talking him into buying sad little trees for his home. She definitely needed to stop kissing him. And she would…

Starting now.

She and Faith had better things to do anyway—namely, getting back to the Christmas festival to get her coveted Santa picture. She'd hoped to get one yesterday, but Faith had decided an early nap was a better use of that time. Candy had already purchased the perfect frame, and it was sitting empty on the mantel, ready and waiting.

"Tonight's the night," she said as she wiped Faith's chubby little hands clean. "It's the last weekend of the Christmas festival and a certain sweet little girl I know is going to get her picture taken on Santa's lap."

Faith gazed up at Candy and smiled wide, eyes sparkling. "Mmm-mmm."

"Mmm-mmm," Candy echoed. "That's right, gingerbread is mmm-mmm good. Now let's get you all dressed and ready. We want to be first in line tonight."

Candy wrestled Faith into a fleece onesie that looked just like Will Ferrell's green costume from the movie *Elf*—her most recent adorable purchase from Melanie's children's boutique. Just as she was placing the matching green-and-yellow hat on Faith's little head, she heard a loud screeching noise that gave her pause.

Faith's eyes went wide.

Candy went still for a second, waiting to see if it happened again. It did, and this time the screech was followed by a few bumps on the wall she shared with Dan. She frowned at the barrier between their living spaces, wondering what could possibly be going on in Dan's half of the duplex.

Never mind. It's not your business, remember?

She turned her attention back to Faith and situated the hat just so. The bell on its pointed top jingled, prompting a string of giggles from the happy baby…until the banging started up again. This time, it was followed by a yelp that definitely sounded like a certain Grinch might be in some sort of trouble.

What in the world?

Whether or not whatever was going on over there was her business, Candy felt like she should check to make sure nothing untoward was happening. She owed Dan that much after all he'd done when she'd taken her spill on the ice.

"We're going to go make sure he's okay because that's what good neighbors do," Candy said as she scooped Faith into her arms and positioned the baby on her hip. "And for no other reason whatsoever."

Faith blinked her big blue eyes. Candy was fairly certain she would have rolled her eyes if that had been something babies do. Thank goodness it wasn't.

Seconds later, she stood on the threshold of

Dan's door—sans welcome mat, because of course he didn't have one—and rang the bell. More banging followed, accompanied by a wail that didn't sound human. Candy was beginning to get seriously concerned. Maybe she should call the firehouse and ask for backup.

But just as she pulled her cell phone from the back pocket of her jeans, the door swung open, revealing a disheveled Dan. Faith babbled with glee at the sight of him, oblivious to his crooked reindeer tie, his half-untucked dress shirt and his perfect Patrick Dempsey hair in a state of clear disarray.

"Yes?" he said, glancing warily over his shoulder before stepping out onto the porch and clicking the door closed behind him.

Something was definitely up.

"Is everything okay? It sounds like you're battling an assassin in there," she said.

Dan snorted as he adjusted his tie. "Close. It's Fancy."

Candy gasped. "You mean the cat that regularly terrorizes the fire department? Are you serious?"

"As a heart attack." He raked a hand through his hair and instantly looked like a candidate for a shampoo commercial. Damn him. "I helped the LFD get her out of Ethel Monroe's sugar maple tree earlier, and somehow that little good deed ended with me agreeing to take her in for the holidays while Ethel goes to visit her grandkids in Florida."

Candy tried her best to wrap her head around what he was saying. He was kitty-sitting an elderly woman's notoriously ferocious beast for Christmas? How very…un-Scroogey of him.

"I need to see this cat." She shoved her cell phone into his hands and reached for the doorknob.

"Candy, I don't think that's a very good idea." Dan moved to stop her, but he was a beat too late.

She'd already flung the door open and entered his side of the house.

"Fancy is dangerous. I really don't want you or Faith to get hurt," Dan said as he attempted to wave her back outside.

No way. She really wanted to get a glimpse of Lovestruck's most dangerous animal.

Plus, now that she was standing in Dan's living room, she could see the stocking she'd made after knitting class hanging from his mantel. It looked every bit as silly as she remembered, yet there it hung.

She looked from the stocking to Dan, unable to stop a smile from spreading across her face.

"What?" he said, shutting the door and coming to stand beside her.

You're just neighbors, remember? Regular, nonkissing neighbors.

She cleared her throat. "Nothing. Now where's this famous cat?"

"Infamous," Dan corrected as he removed his tie and unbuttoned the top button of his shirt. Candy did her best not to stare. How was it possible that a tiny sliver of exposed skin at the base of a man's neck could be so mesmerizing? "There's a difference."

"Right." What were they talking about, again? Oh yeah, the cat.

She bounced Faith on her hip and glanced around the room until she finally spotted a ball of gray fur balanced at the tiptop of the little tree that she'd forced on Dan at the Christmas tree farm. The tree stood in the center of his coffee table with a single red ornament dangling from one of its boughs in true Charlie Brown style. No garland, no silver strands of icicles, no lights. Not even a tree skirt. The only other item on the modest fir tree's limbs was the adorable kitten clinging to the top branch like she was a living, breathing tree topper.

"Oh my gosh." Candy pressed her free hand to her chest. "Look at her. She's precious."

The cat blinked her pretty blue eyes. Faith waved at the animal and Fancy's fluffy tail swished back and forth.

"This can't be the same cat that put Jack Cole in the hospital." Candy shook her head. "No possible way."

She took a step toward the kitty. Dan grabbed her hand and reeled her back to his side just as Fancy swiped at the air with a paw. An ear-splitting meow followed.

Faith's eyes went huge.

Candy winced. "Okay, I'm beginning to see the problem."

"Yeah." Dan blew out a breath. His gaze remained glued to the cat as he kept a loose hold on her hand.

Then his fingers wove themselves tenderly through hers and she went a little breathless.

"I thought Fancy liked you," she whispered.

"She does." Dan nodded. "She's just having a little trouble adjusting to the change of scenery. I'm sure she'll settle down."

Candy studied him, marveling at his ability

to look at his current situation and interpret the look in Fancy's icy gaze as anything but polite disdain.

"Oh my gosh, you're a good person," she blurted.

"What?" He glanced at her, taking in the ridiculous grin on her face that seemed to be growing wider by the second. Then, as if by instinct, he dropped her hand and crossed his arms.

Candy rolled her eyes. "You can pretend all you want, but your secret is out. You, Dan Manning, are a good and decent person."

Fancy meowed again as she circled the top of the little tree and did her best to disappear among its meager branches. Dan sighed. Candy pressed her lips together in an effort to keep from laughing out loud, but it was no use. A giggle escaped her, and Faith immediately echoed the laugh.

Dan glared at them both.

"Oh come on, you talk a big Grinchy game, but deep down, you're nothing but a giant softie. Who else would volunteer for the most dreaded pet-sitting job in all of Lovestruck?" Candy waved a hand at the tree, where Fancy had wrapped herself so snugly around its trunk that the tiny Scotch pine looked as if it sported two piercing blue eyes. "Possibly the entirety of Vermont."

"It's nothing," he said through clenched teeth.

"On the contrary, it's a big, giant something." She gave him a little shoulder bump. "Admit you're a good man. You just like to pretend otherwise during the holidays, for reasons unknown."

His gaze shifted toward hers until their eyes locked. And the soulful way he looked at her made all of her breath bottle up in her throat. Why did he suddenly seem so familiar—like they'd known each other for years…since those innocent days when Christmas was as pure and perfect as December's first snowfall?

Memories moved behind his eyes, and she wished he would share them with her. She wished it so, so much. She wanted to know him. *Really* know him. She was even willing to forget the fact that she'd kissed him and he'd fled, leaving her with the shattered pieces of a glass heart at her feet. If only he'd just open up to her…

"I'm not that good," he said in a rumbly, masculine voice that made her tummy flip.

Faith's head dropped onto Candy's shoulder

and she closed her eyes. Dan rested his palm on her tiny back. His hand seemed comically big by comparison, as if he could prop up Candy and Faith's whole world…cradle both of their lost hearts in his strong grasp.

"Dan," she whispered, his name a plea. A promise.

He exhaled a ragged breath and cupped the back of her head with a feather-light touch. Candy leaned into it, like a flower pushing through snow in search of sunshine.

Dan rested his forehead against hers, and they stayed like that for several long moments. So close, so *very* close to kissing again that Candy could taste it, feel it—the warmth of his mouth moving against hers, sweet like peppermint, while snow gathered in her eyelashes, her hair…

And then Candy's phone rang, jarring them both back to the present.

Dan shook his head as if rousing himself from a dream. A tinny, distorted version of Mariah Carey's "All I Want for Christmas Is You" blared from his left hand. It sounded like the world's most annoying alarm clock.

What the—?

He took a backward step away from Candy and glanced down. Her phone was still gripped tightly in his palm after she'd shoved it at him when she'd been so intent on storming her way inside to see the cat. Candy was sneaky that way, he'd come to realize. Always worming her way into places she didn't belong by virtue of her charm, optimism and sheer force of will. His town. His home. His life.

My heart, he thought with no small amount of regret.

No matter how many times he reminded himself that he couldn't do this, didn't *want* to do this, it kept happening. His hands kept burying themselves in her soft, lush hair and his lips kept seeking hers. Wishing…wanting… wanting so damn much. Wanting everything— every cheery, Christmas-loving part of her, no matter how much it hurt.

Mariah kept singing about the one and only thing she needed for Christmas, oblivious to Dan's inner turmoil. *Of course* this sappy holiday song was Candy's ringtone. She'd probably used it year-round.

"Um, I think my phone is ringing," Candy said, glancing from Dan to the device and back again.

"Right." He nodded and glanced at the

phone's display. A man's name flashed across the screen.

Gabe.

Dan's chest went tight, like it did every time he thought about Candy teaming up with one of the firefighters at the relay race last night at the party after his departure. If he didn't know better, he would have thought he was jealous.

Denial much? You are *jealous.*

"It's Gabe," he said, offering Candy the phone.

"Oh!" She beamed all of a sudden, and Dan felt like he could barely breathe. "Do you mind if I take this? It's my boss."

So this mysterious Gabe person was her boss. Of course, that didn't necessarily mean that Candy didn't have a special someone waiting for her back home, but Dan felt a telltale loosening in the tense set of his shoulders all the same.

"Don't mind a bit." He reached for the baby. "I can watch Faith while you talk to him."

"Thanks." Candy tapped the screen to accept the call while Faith snuggled into the crook of Dan's elbow. "Hello?"

Dan thought he should probably give Candy some space, even though the call was professional rather than personal. So he carried Faith into the kitchen and began filling the coffeepot with water. A dose of caffeine was definitely in order so long as he was on high alert for Fancy-related disasters.

Alas, his modest little cottage didn't afford much privacy, given that it had been split into two residences. As soon as he turned off the faucet, Candy's voice rang through the space like a sweet, silvery bell.

"Gabe, it's so great to hear from you. I was beginning to wonder if you'd gotten my messages."

Dan rocked Faith from side to side while he scooped coffee grounds into the filter with his free hand. So Candy had been trying to reach her boss? Interesting.

"What do you think that's all about?" he whispered to Faith.

She blinked her big blue eyes.

Great. He was gossiping with an infant. At what point, exactly, had he morphed into Frances?

"Forget I asked. It's none of my business," he said to the baby.

Her tiny rosebud mouth spread into a happy grin, despite the solemnity in his tone.

"We understand each other, don't we?" He winked, and Faith let out a giggle.

Despite this ongoing exchange, Dan kept catching snippets of Candy's conversation from the other room. He heard words like *centered* and *focused* sprinkled among all the complimentary things she said about Lovestruck. And then, just as the coffeepot was filled to the brim, she said something that made his stomach plummet.

"The day after Christmas? That soon, huh?"

Dan's hand paused midway to the cabinet where he kept the coffee mugs.

"Um, sure. I could be there by the twenty-sixth, if you really need me right away," Candy said, more quietly this time.

Dan turned around to rest against the kitchen counter as he strained to listen. Faith wrapped her delicate fist around one of his fingers.

The twenty-sixth? That couldn't be right, could it? Candy had rented the duplex through the first of the year.

"I'm sure. You just caught me off guard. I'm ready to get back to work. Truly," she said. "I'll probably have to leave on Christmas Day, but that's okay. Faith will still have time to open her gifts and celebrate Christmas morning."

Was it just wishful thinking, or was there a hint of hesitancy in her tone?

"No, absolutely not." This time, her voice was laced with a sadness that seemed to scrape Dan's insides. It was unmistakable. "There's nothing keeping me here."

He froze, jaw clenching so hard that his teeth ached.

"I've got everything under control. Just send me the details once all the arrangements have been made," Candy said, all business. "Thanks so much, Gabe. Things will be different after Christmas. I promise."

Dan exhaled a tense breath. *Things will be different after Christmas.*

They certainly would. But he had only himself to blame for that, didn't he? He'd pushed Candy away at each and every turn, and now she was all set to give him exactly what he wanted—she was leaving ahead of schedule.

He should've been relieved. But as he turned around and reached into the cabinet for two coffee cups, an overwhelming sense of loss came over him. He had to work to keep his hand steady as he set the mugs gently on the countertop, one by one.

In the other room, Candy ended the call.

There was a prolonged pause before she breezed into the kitchen with her trademark smile dancing on her lips. But it didn't quite seem to reach her eyes this time.

"You made coffee," she said quietly.

She smelled like warm gingerbread, just as she had when she'd walked inside his home a half hour ago, wrapping him up in a heady cloud of sugar and spice. But the sweet intimacy that had developed between them was no longer there. Candy seemed to be looking anywhere and everywhere besides at Dan. And he no longer knew what to say or how to act.

She was leaving…on Christmas Day. How was that possible?

"Would you like some?" Dan poured a cup of coffee and offered it to Candy.

She took it, and when her fingertips brushed against his, time seemed to stand still. She gave him a wobbly smile. "You didn't happen to pick up any of that peppermint patty creamer I mentioned, did you?"

As a matter of fact, he had. He'd been grocery shopping at Village Market and it had practically leaped straight into his basket.

"Perhaps." He shrugged one shoulder.

"That seems an awful lot like something

a good man would do," Candy said. Her eyes went shiny, as if she might be holding back tears.

"Maybe I just had a craving," he countered.

"Liar."

So this was how it was going to be? She wasn't going to say anything to him about her new plans. They were going to dance around the truth and pretend everything was fine.

Dan shouldn't have been surprised. Isn't that what he'd been doing all along—dancing around the truth of how he felt about her? Side-stepping memories that had the power to turn back time, all because he'd been sleepwalking his way through the holidays for so long that he was afraid to wake up?

Candy didn't owe him an explanation. She didn't owe him a thing. In fact, the very opposite was true.

She brushed past him, removed the creamer from the fridge and poured an absurdly huge dollop of it into her mug. Dan's teeth hurt just watching her coffee go from bitter black to a blond hue a shade or two lighter than the curls that tumbled down her back. Then she took a sip and released a dreamy sigh that made his heart twist in his chest. Faith's grip tightened around his finger, as if she never wanted to let go, and the twist turned into a dull, throbbing ache.

"Want some?" Candy moved to attack his perfectly acceptable cup of black coffee with the tooth-rotting concoction that had recently taken up residence in his Frigidaire.

He covered the top of his mug with his free hand. "No, thanks. I think I'll pass."

She gazed at him over the top of her cup, eyes shining bright. "You honestly don't know what you're missing."

Not true. The same decades-old weight settled on Dan's heart, but now it seemed heavier than ever before. Crushing, almost. *Christmas isn't even over, and I already know exactly what...and who... I'll miss most of all.*

Chapter Twelve

Candy wrestled with her crochet hook a few days later during her holiday craft class at Main Street Yarn. Today's lesson involved crocheting festive pot holders, which were infinitely simpler to make than Christmas stockings. She just wasn't sure when she'd ever get the chance to use them since she'd yet to master even the simplest cookie recipe or ramshackle gingerbread house. And now that she was due to leave Lovestruck right after Christmas morning, time was running out.

"Good job, Candy." Alice nodded at the wobbly square in Candy's hands. At least it was recognizable as a valid shape, unlike the tangle of yarn that was currently hanging from Dan's mantel.

"Thank you," Candy said around the lump in her throat.

The lump had lodged itself there shortly after the call from Gabe a few days ago. It was silly, really. She'd never asked to take off for the holidays. She'd been distraught at the prospect at first. Bringing Faith to Lovestruck and coming up with a Christmas to-do list had been an act of desperation more than any real holiday planning on Candy's part. A way to forget that she'd been temporarily fired.

If Gabe had summoned her back to California on her very first day in Vermont, she would have gladly skipped out of town without even unpacking her suitcases. But now, every time she thought about leaving for good, she sort of wanted to load up everyone and everything in Lovestruck and take them home with her.

Starting with Dan.

Of course, any attempt to drag him to California would probably need to involve straight-up kidnapping, because the man clearly had zero interest in accompanying her anywhere.

Candy was certain he'd overheard her conversation with Gabe the other day. Dan's cottage was cozy. *Intimate*, which Candy positively adored, but it didn't afford much privacy for vacation-altering phone calls.

He hadn't uttered a word about her change in plans. Not immediately after she'd gotten off the phone with Gabe and not in the days since. Not even after she'd tacked a note to his door informing him that she would now be leaving on Christmas Day—a move necessitated by the fact that she hadn't set eyes on him in days. Either he was planning on going into full-on hermit mode to get through the remainder of the holidays or Fancy had murdered him in his sleep. Candy wasn't sure which theory she preferred.

She just felt so stupid. So hurt. Which was utterly ridiculous, considering that she and Dan were wholly incompatible. But when she'd discovered that he'd bought her favorite coffee creamer, her heart had turned to mush right inside her chest. It seemed significant.

Apparently not, though, since he'd since ghosted her like he was Jacob Marley and she was Ebenezer Scrooge.

Ha. She jabbed her crochet hook into her

yarn. *As if.* If anyone was Scrooge in this scenario, it was Dan. Obviously.

"Candy?" Madison arched a brow at her from across the table. "Did that pot holder do something to deserve your wrath, or are you just in a bad mood today?"

Felicity, Melanie and Alice all turned to look at Candy. Her face went warm. She supposed she could officially add *pot holder murderer* to her résumé now, along with *bad knitter, sloppy skater, burner of cookies* and *ruiner of Christmas.*

"I'm not in a bad mood," she said.

Never in Candy's life had anyone asked her that question before. Candy wasn't a moody person. She was an optimist. Or, as Gabe had always called her, a "romantic." A true-blue glass-half-full type of person. In short, the very opposite of Dan Manning and his temporary feline tenant.

"I've just got a lot on my mind, that's all." She glanced around the table at the kind faces staring back at her.

She really liked these women—all of them. In the short time she'd been in Lovestruck, they'd become more than just acquaintances. They were her friends. Those moments when she'd thought otherwise at the LFD Christmas party, she'd been lying to herself. Again, she blamed Dan. Men shouldn't be allowed to kiss a woman silly and then refuse to run around the room with her with an ornament on a spoon.

You kissed *him, remember?*

Candy swallowed and banished the memory from her mind, yet again. She needed to tell her friends that she was going home ahead of schedule. Since the call from Gabe, she'd been doing nothing but packing and procrastinating. Right now, though, it was time to face the music and announce she was leaving early.

"I hope everything is okay, dear." Alice reached to give Candy's non-crochet-hook-holding hand a squeeze. "You know we're here if you ever need anything."

Candy took a deep breath. Ugh, this was going to be even harder than she'd thought. "Thank you so much. You're all so nice, and you've made Faith and me feel right at home here. It's been wonderful."

She glanced down at Faith, grinning happily from a bouncy seat that Madison had brought to the yarn shop, insisting that any baby who sat in it would stop crying in a millisecond. She hadn't been wrong. Candy would need to get one when she got back home. It would be perfect to use on set.

Gabe won't let you bring Faith to work anymore. That's the whole reason you got fired in the first place.

Right. No bouncy seat, then.

"I got a call from my boss the other day, and it looks like I need to cut my vacation short," she said.

"Oh, no." Alice pressed a hand to her chest. "That's too bad. You and Faith have had such a nice holiday here in Lovestruck."

Candy felt herself getting misty-eyed. They had, hadn't they? All domestic failures aside.

"When do you have to go?" Madison set down her perfectly crafted pot holder. Maybe if Candy moved here, she'd eventually possess stellar yarn skills. "I hope it's not before New Year's Eve. The *Bee* throws a great party in one of the old covered bridges with homemade hot chocolate and fireworks at midnight. You have to come."

That sounded all kinds of adorable. Candy might even have to steal the idea for a future work project.

Maybe not, though. Mining Lovestruck traditions and broadcasting them into people's living rooms felt wrong somehow.

"I wish I could, but I'm booked on a flight out of Burlington on Christmas Day."

"Christmas Day?" Felicity gaped at her. "You're kidding, right?"

"I wish, but no. We begin filming a new movie on the twenty-sixth. I begged my boss to put me on the next project. Multiple times, actually. I really need to show up and do good work." Candy didn't elaborate. She doubted people in Lovestruck would understand why bringing a baby to work with you would end badly when everyone in town seemed to be pushing a baby stroller. Or in Madison's case, a *double* stroller.

"That's so sad." Felicity shook her head.

"Definitely not ideal," Melanie said. "But we'll just have to make the best of it. Or try to, anyway."

Madison winced. "Yeah, that's going to be tough, considering."

Candy felt herself frown. "Considering what?"

"The storm, honey. Surely you've heard that Lovestruck is under a winter storm advisory," Alice said.

Candy, in fact, had not been privy to this information. Perhaps if she hadn't been too busy figuring out if she needed an entire suitcase solely dedicated to Faith's new winter wardrobe and whom she might hire to remove half a dozen Christmas trees from the duplex after she left, she might have been more up to speed on current weather phenomena.

"I had no idea. How bad of a storm are we talking about?"

Madison winced. "The weather reporter at the *Bee* says we could get at least a foot of snow and most likely much more."

Candy gulped. That sounded like an enormous amount of snow. "I guess I need to get down to the Christmas festival tonight to get Faith's Santa picture before the weather gets bad."

"I'm afraid you can't." Felicity shook her head. "The festival has been canceled, starting tonight. The mayor wants everyone to stay home and safe until the weather system passes."

"Wait." Candy cast a longing glance out the window. There wasn't a camel in sight, darn it. "Completely canceled? All of it? But it's not even snowing."

Melanie shot Candy a meaningful look. "*Yet.*

Honey, this is Vermont. We don't cancel much for snow, but we aren't foolish either."

Candy was aware. If she'd forgotten where she was, the signs advertising maple syrup, maple lattes and maple candy would have reminded her in a hurry.

"It snows here. A lot. And by all accounts, we've got heaps of it coming our way tonight." Felicity bit her lip. "Do you have any idea how to prepare for a snowstorm?"

"Zero," Candy said flatly. "I'm from California, remember?"

She was also used to film-set life, where she didn't need to worry about anything but work. The production company that financed Gabe's films provided for her basic needs, just like it did for everyone else on the crew. Food, lodging, all of it. In any given year, she spent more nights in hotels than she did in her own condo. Which meant she hardly ever even had to clean up after herself, much less prepare for an imminent natural disaster.

Was it any wonder she still couldn't make a simple batch of Christmas cookies?

"It's going to be fine. You just need to stock up on basic necessities in case you get stuck inside for a few days," Alice said.

"A few *days*?" Candy shook her head.

No.

No, no, no.

Christmas was right around the corner. She needed her Santa picture, although at the moment, that seemed like it might be the least of her problems.

"But I'm supposed to be going back home on Christmas Day," she said.

More importantly, she couldn't be trapped in a house with Dan for an unknown number of days. Not even a house that was technically split down the middle. He hadn't even bothered to knock on her door to warn her about the blizzard.

Maybe he was rooting for her to be buried alive in an avalanche so she'd stop pestering him with inflatable reindeer and poorly knit stockings.

Nice try, Ebenezer.

No way was she going to let that happen. She could totally survive a blizzard…on her own…with a baby. Even though she knew nothing about snowstorms and still felt like she was faking her way through motherhood.

"Dan is great at this sort of thing. I'm sure he's prepared the house. You don't need to worry about anything except taking care of Faith," Felicity said.

It was a wonder how everyone in Lovestruck seemed to think that Dan was the nicest guy in the entire world. He must undergo a complete personality transplant every January.

Then again, Candy had gotten a few glimpses of Dan's inner nice guy lately. Make no mistake, there was definitely a good man lurking there somewhere beneath the novelty ties and December scowl…a man who had a tendency to make her go all swoony when she least expected it.

"Dr. Manning will be there to help in case you need anything," someone said.

Candy's head snapped up and she took in the sight of nurse Frances, Dan's right-hand woman, browsing the aisles of yarn. How had Candy failed to notice her? The Elf crocs alone should have made her impossible to overlook.

"Hi, Frances." Candy commanded her brain to stop thinking about him in such glowing terms, lest Frances's talents included mind reading along with having her medically trained finger constantly on the pulse of the town's rumor mill. "I'm sure you're right. Dan—er, Dr. Manning— is a great landlord. Very thorough."

Thoroughly maddening.

"He sure is. And he's nicer than he lets on." Frances made a big show of looking over her shoulder in case anyone might be spying on them. "He's even adopting Ethel Monroe's cat. Permanently. But you didn't hear that from me."

"Fancy?" Candy felt her mouth drop open. "I thought he was just pet-sitting her for the holidays."

"So does Dr. Manning. But Ethel just signed a lease on a new apartment down there in Florida. It's one of those high-end independent living places. No pets allowed." Frances mimed locking her mouth with an invisible key. "But again, you didn't hear it from me."

Candy bit back a laugh. The thought of Dan living with Fancy permanently was almost enough to make her forget about the weather entirely.

"Can I help you find something, Frances?" Alice said, deftly putting an end to any further gossip.

Felicity generously offered to babysit Faith the following day so Candy could finish packing. Candy took her up on it, and then she stowed her crochet project and headed home to figure out how to survive a Vermont snowstorm.

Lucky for her, Dan was more than willing to mansplain to her how to do just that.

"Hey there," he said as she walked up the path to the house. He'd been poised to knock on her door when she'd rounded the corner, pushing Faith's stroller.

"Hi," Candy said, stopping short of asking him if he'd been avoiding her.

"Listen, we're probably going to be getting some snow soon." He scrubbed the back of his neck as if he'd rather have been anywhere than here, having this conversation with her. "Tomorrow night, in fact."

How sweet. Apparently he did care if she lived or died. "I just heard."

"Good." He nodded. "Under the circumstances, I think it would be best if you and Faith come stay in my half of the house."

She gaped at him. He couldn't be serious.

"I know I'm right next door, but I'd feel better if you were under my side of the roof. I know this weather. You don't." He smiled. "You'd save me from getting up every hour to check on you. Agreed?"

What?

No.

Don't agree! Do not.

She had to stop herself from actually laughing out loud. "Thanks, but no. I've got everything under control. It's just a little snow."

Listen to her—she sounded just like a real Vermonter. *What's a foot or so of white stuff during the holidays?*

Dan narrowed his gaze at her. "So you know to drip the faucets to keep the pipes from freezing?"

Candy nodded. "Sure do." She knew now that he'd mentioned it, anyway.

"I still don't like idea of you and Faith being on your own," he said.

"We'll be fine, I promise." Definitely more fine than she'd be if she had to move in with Dan.

What if she accidentally kissed him again?

Her face went warm just thinking about it.

"Are you okay?" Dan said. "You look a little pale."

"I'm fine. Everything is great." She hustled toward her half of the duplex. "See you around. Have a great blizzard!"

She waved at him as she ushered Faith inside and shut the door.

Have a great blizzard? Really?

Chapter Thirteen

The following night, Candy went to sleep expecting to wake up to a snowy white Christmas Eve. When she put on her red plaid pajamas and climbed into bed, the snow was already coming down in huge, fat flakes. Out her bedroom window, all she could see was a flurry of white—like feathers shaken from an angelic pillow fight.

Somewhere in the back of her head, she wondered if the storm might affect her travel plans for Christmas Day. Surely not. As everyone at the yarn store had said, this was Vermont. They were used to snow here.

Besides, if she *did* happen to get stuck in Lovestruck, perhaps it would be fate's way of stepping in and letting her know that she was right where she was supposed to be. That was the ultimate message of all those snowed-in-at-Christmas movies she'd worked on, wasn't it?

Candy had a strange feeling in the pit of her stomach thinking about it, though. She couldn't possibly stay in Vermont permanently. Forever was a mighty long time. Anyone would have fallen under the spell of Lovestruck during the holidays. But even amid the splendor of its small-town Christmas charm, she'd still messed everything up. Case in point: she'd eaten half a stale gingerbread house for dinner, and Faith wasn't going to have a Santa picture to remember her very first Christmas. Every time she'd tried to make the Santa photo happen, something got in the way.

Of all the things that had gone wrong during this forced vacation, that glaring omission had to be the worst. Candy could have easily gotten Faith's photo taken with Santa at the local shopping mall back home. But, no. She'd traveled clear across the country in search of a perfect Christmas and ended up with a mess on her hands…not to mention a heart that felt like it just might be breaking.

If that wasn't fate's way of telling her she needed to get on the first plane out of town, she didn't know what was.

Of course, she still had to get through the rest of Christmas first. The presents she'd picked up in her shopping sprees were all wrapped and tucked under the living room tree, and the refrigerator was stocked with everything she needed in order to duplicate—ineptly, no doubt—the Christmas Day breakfast her mom had always made when she was a kid. Buttermilk pancakes made in three different sizes and arranged on a plate to resemble a snowman. Two green M&M's for eyes, strawberry buttons and a jaunty scarf crafted from two strips of bacon. Maple bacon in this case, because for now, they were still in Vermont. Her mom had always dusted the pancake snowman with powdered sugar and piled the bottom of the plate with whipped cream to look like snow. Candy could see it in her mind as clearly as if it had happened yesterday…before that last Christmas trip to Lovestruck, before the gazebo, before the accident.

Looking back, Candy's life had always felt like it had been split in two—before she'd lost her parents and after. That long-ago Christmas Eve in the gazebo had been the last time she could remember being truly happy, oblivious to the many ways that life could hurt. It had been the Christmas of her first kiss and also the last holiday she'd ever spend with her family—a first and last Christmas, all wrapped up in one heartbreaking package.

Now that she had one foot back in LA, Candy realized that returning to Lovestruck after so many years hadn't just been about giving Faith a perfect Christmas. It had also been her way of trying to stitch her life back together, to join the two halves into a whole so she could be a proper mother for Faith. She'd been chasing the magic of Christmas for her entire career and still hadn't managed to find it. If she couldn't heal in Lovestruck, maybe she never would. Maybe Faith would simply have to grow up with empty frames on the mantel and a mom who couldn't actually knit.

Candy just needed to get through the rest of the holidays and hightail it back to real life.

She squeezed her eyes closed tight and waited for sleep to come. *Since when did Christmas be-*

come something you need to force yourself "to get through"? Her eyes flew open.

Her inner thoughts were starting to sound an awful lot like Dan. If that wasn't a frightening realization, nothing was.

She blamed the kiss. What a mistake that had been. Not only had it left her feeling like she was halfway in love with him, he'd somehow kissed the Christmas spirit right out of her.

Anyway, she was *not* half in love with him. At least that's what she tried to tell herself as her eyes drifted back shut and she let the pitter-patter of snow against glass lull her into a deep, dark sleep.

Hours later—or possibly minutes, since she was so disoriented that it was hard to tell how much time had passed—it wasn't the storm that woke her up. Nor was it the chill that had descended on her cozy little bedroom and caused her to burrow deep under the covers in her sleep. Instead, she was jolted in wakefulness by earsplitting cries coming from Faith's bedroom.

Candy knew immediately that something was wrong. Weeks ago, when she'd first brought Faith home, the baby routinely woke up in the middle of the night. Candy had spent hours rocking her back to sleep and crying along with her, convinced that Faith missed her real parents and knew deep down that she'd been left with a pale imitation of what a mother should be.

But after a few days, things had calmed down. The first night that Faith slept through the night, Candy had wondered if it was just a fluke. But then one night had turned into two, two into three, and Candy finally started yawning a little bit less at work. Although, she was still reluctant to leave Faith with a sitter and interrupt their bonding process—hence, the BabyBjörn and Candy's subsequent firing.

These cries were different, though. They weren't fussy mews of discomfort, confusion or hunger. Faith's wails seemed to scream of urgency, punctuated by panicked gulps of air.

Please. Candy kicked furiously as she tried to disentangle herself from the pile of blankets. *Please let her be okay.*

She stumbled out of bed, nearly crashing into the nightstand. The room was so pitch-black that she couldn't see her hand in front of her face. Why was it so dark?

Her heart beat a panicked rhythm as she fumbled for her phone, so she could light the way to Faith's room. She'd slept in so many hotels over the years on location that she knew better than to stumble her way through the dark in a place that wasn't her real home. But Dan's duplex had little night-lights in every room. She loved those tiny lights.

Faith's cries intensified as Candy realized that the power must have gone out in the storm. No wonder she was so cold. If she'd been able to see anything, every breath she took probably would have been visible as a misty cloud, suspended midair.

"It's okay, sweetheart," she called as she finally grabbed hold of her phone. "I'm coming. Everything's okay. It's just a storm."

The time on her phone read three in the morning, and a missed notification popped up on the screen as she swiped on the flashlight.

Weather Advisory: A blizzard warning is in effect for your area. Please take necessary precautions.

A blizzard? She was in an actual *blizzard* right now? That sounded a whole lot worse than a winter storm, for some reason. And what precautions? Candy didn't have a clue how to prepare for a blizzard.

Also, wasn't it a tad too late for warnings? She'd already lost heat and electricity and she had a terrified baby on her hands.

Teeth chattering, she ran to Faith's room, holding out her phone in front of her to light the way. When she flung the door open, the baby's cries seemed to double in volume. Candy couldn't even think. By rote, she flipped the light switch on but, of course, nothing happened.

"I'm here. I'm here, love bug. Everything is fine," she whispered, hoping a soothing tone would help calm Faith down. But even Candy could hear the tremor of fear in her own voice. Were they really safe? How long would it be before the power came back on? People couldn't live without heat in this sort of weather, could they?

She set the phone down on a nearby table and reached into the bassinet, scooping Faith into her arms. But instead of melting into Candy's embrace like she usually did, Faith's tiny body stiffened. Her hands balled into angry fists. She was crying so hard that she was shaking all over.

"Oh my gosh, you're burning up." Candy bit down hard on her lip. This couldn't be good. The room was freezing, and Faith's skin was hot to the touch.

She pressed Faith into her shoulder and tried

doing the bouncy thing she loved so much. She tried rocking from side to side. Nothing seemed to calm the baby down, and Faith's forehead was so warm that Candy could feel it through the plaid fabric of her pajamas.

"Okay, it's got to be a fever," Candy said. "That's okay. We can figure this out. Of course we can."

She was pretty sure she had baby Tylenol in her mommy-and-me first aid kit. A thermometer, too. Beyond those items, she didn't know what she might need. But that was okay, because she had the internet. Candy could just do a search for how to bring down a fever in a baby.

There was no reason to panic. Sure, the lack of power was a problem, but babies had been getting fevers since the olden times. Google would tell her what to do, right?

Wrong. The Wi-Fi was down, of course. A house without electricity couldn't power a modem. Her data plan wasn't working properly either, probably due to the storm. Every time she typed something into a search bar, the wheel on her screen went round and round while Faith cried and cried. And with each passing second, the battery life bar on Candy's phone got smaller and smaller.

Her phone couldn't die. She needed that flashlight, and her small handheld device was her only connection to the outside world at the moment, even if it wasn't exactly in prime working condition.

"First things first," Candy cooed to Faith. "We need to get some baby Tylenol in you and then we'll light a fire in the fireplace."

Candy was no Girl Scout, but there was a big stack of wood under a tarp on the side of the house. She'd seen one of those lighters with the long nozzles in a drawer someplace in the kitchen. Humans had been making fires since the Stone Age. How hard could it be?

She carried Faith to the bathroom and managed to find the first aid kit. Given the circumstances, the fact that the battery seemed to be working in the thermometer felt like a miracle. Candy sent up a silent prayer of thanks...

Until she saw the reading on the thermometer's tiny digital display.

"One hundred and two?" she said, voice breaking on a sob.

Faith's cries had gotten softer, quieter, but she let loose with another wail at the sound of the raw emotion in Candy's voice.

"No, no, no, love bug. Try not to cry. It will

only make you feel worse." She was outright begging now, but what else was she supposed to do?

She tried to think back and remember the times when she'd been sick as a kid. Her mom had always been the best at making her feel better. The first time she'd gotten sick with a stomach flu after her parents passed away, she was certain she'd die too without her mom there to hold back her hair and press a cool washcloth to her forehead.

Right…a washcloth!

Candy held Faith close with one arm and reached into the cabinet for a clean, fluffy face towel. She tossed it in the sink, turned on the faucet and…

…nothing happened. Not a single drop of water came flowing out of the spout. Candy just stared at it in the darkness, trying to make sense out of what was happening.

Oh, no. It's the pipes, isn't it? They're frozen.

She bit her lip to keep from crying. Faith already had enough tears streaming down her face for the both of them.

But this was all Candy's fault, wasn't it? She'd forgotten to drip the faucets, even after Dan had warned that the pipes could freeze.

He was probably going to give her zero stars on Airbnb and insist on keeping her security deposit.

Not that she cared. She had way bigger problems at the moment than her rating on a travel app. At the rate things were going, she might not even be around to see her terrible Airbnb rating. She'd made a mess out of Christmas and now she'd done far worse.

She'd made a mess out of motherhood.

"I'm sorry," she said, wiping Faith's tears with the soft, dry cloth. "I'm so sorry, baby. I'll get us out of this mess, I promise I will."

Dan woke to the sound of pounding on his front door.

At first, he assumed the racket was Fancy's doing. As Dan had discovered over the course of the past few nights, the cat possessed some strong nocturnal tendencies.

More than once, he'd woken up in the wee hours of the morning to find the fluffy kitty situated dead in the center of his chest, appraising him with icy blue eyes. The first time it happened, it had nearly given Dan a heart attack. He'd since found it preferable to being roused by Fancy's late-night antics in the kitchen—

including, but not limited to, batting around an entire foil-wrapped pie that Frances had baked for him, ripping open a loaf of bread and shredding it to crumbs in true Hansel and Gretel fashion, and shutting herself into the cabinet where Dan kept the cat food. How long had she been in there before she'd started yowling for help?

More than long enough to polish off the entire bag of Meow Mix.

"Fancy, go back to sleep," Dan yelled, flipping to his opposite side in bed. In the process, his hand brushed against a warm lump of fur.

He sat up. "Fancy?"

The cat was curled into a tight ball, nestled beside him in the bed. This was certainly new... and surprisingly sweet. But if the knocking he'd heard hadn't been Fancy, then what was it?

Bang, bang, bang.

There it was again, and now that Dan was awake—mostly—he could hear someone calling his name.

Candy. He bolted out of bed, shot straight through with adrenaline. He wasn't sure how he knew it was her. He just knew.

Besides, who else would be trying to beat down his door in the middle of a snowstorm?

He bolted down the hall toward the entryway, bare feet slapping against the cold wood floor. Why was it so freaking cold? And why couldn't he see anything? The hallway was dark as pitch.

Fancy darted in front of him—because of course she did—and he stumbled into a wall. That's when he realized that the power had gone out. No heat, no electricity.

No wonder Candy had come knocking.

He should have insisted that she and Faith stay with him until the snowstorm passed. He'd tried...but not hard enough. She hadn't wanted to stay with him in his half of the duplex, and like an idiot, he'd taken it personally. It was one of many mistakes he'd made lately, all where Candy was concerned.

If Dan had still been a kid...

If he'd still believed in the wonder of Christmas and things like midnight snowfalls and fateful moments in the most unlikely of places...

If he'd been able to go back to the gazebo again—*all* the way back...

He would have made a Christmas wish—a wish for another chance with Candy. A chance to do things differently.

But that wasn't possible, obviously. Second chances only came around in the sort of movies that Candy loved so much. He wasn't about to go backward in time or wake up in the same bed on the same morning again and again, *Groundhog Day*–style, until he finally managed to get things right.

All Dan had was this week, this day, this Christmas. Saddest of all, it wasn't even over yet, but he'd already lost his chance. He'd lost Candy. In less than forty-eight hours, she'd be gone and everything in Lovestruck would go back to normal.

Just like you wanted... You've been waiting for January all this time. And now it's come even sooner than you expected.

In the darkness, he fumbled with the lock as cold air crept through the sliver of space in the doorframe. He blamed his melancholy on the bitter cold and the late hour. Didn't things always seem more dire in the middle of the night?

But when he flung the door open and caught sight of Candy standing on his threshold, knee-deep in the snow that had blown drifts on the porch, with tears streaming down her face and a weepy baby in her arms, a chill coursed through him that had nothing to do with the storm. A more dire sight, he'd never witnessed.

"I'm sorry." She flashed him a valiant attempt at a smile, but it slid right off of her face. "I know it's late and you were probably sleeping, but Faith is sick and there's no heat or water. And I—"

"Come here," Dan said, pulling them both into his arms. The way she clung to him—as if he had all the answers, as if he could make everything right, which Dan knew all too well he couldn't—should have made him shut down, like he always did when emotions became too much for him to handle. He was just a man, after all. A man who'd already spent most of his life trying to atone for the mistakes of his youth, but never feeling like it was enough.

Would it *ever* be enough?

"Just come inside, sweetheart," he whispered into her frosty hair.

Then he ushered her into his home and shut the door on the rest of the world while the storm raged on.

Chapter Fourteen

Candy couldn't stop shivering. The distance
from her door to Dan's was only a few feet,
but it may as well have been miles. She felt
like she'd just crossed the length of Antarc-
tica in nothing but her favorite J Crew pajamas
and a pair of woefully inadequate hiking boots.
Whenever she inhaled, it felt like icy pins attacking her nose and throat.

The snow boggled her mind. There was just
so much of it…everywhere. She'd had to use a
shovel just to make a path to Dan's side of the
duplex. It had only taken a matter of minutes,

but her arms ached from the effort as much as her eyes were hurting from the effort it took not to cry.

Not that she was succeeding on that front.

She wiped her face on the sleeve of the fresh pair of pj's that Dan had handed her seconds after he'd hauled her inside. They were soft flannel, and they smelled like clean laundry that had hung outside to dry with just a hint of Dan's woodsy pine scent. She'd climbed right into them, so emotionally and physically exhausted that she could have curled up into a ball right there on the bathroom floor and gone to sleep if she hadn't been so worried about Faith's fever.

"It looks like an ear infection," Dan said, when she came out of the bathroom. Faith rubbed one of her eyes with a tiny fist and yawned as he held her against his chest. "She was tugging on her left ear while she was crying, and you're right. She's got a fever. You said you already gave her some baby Tylenol?"

"Yes, just a few minutes ago." Candy nodded, feeling like a child herself in Dan's oversize nightclothes. The sleeves reached down to her fingertips and the thick felt slippers he'd given her had to be at least three sizes too big.

An ear infection. It seemed so obvious. How had Candy not known that's what was happening? She'd seen Faith playing with her ear right before she'd fallen asleep and hadn't thought anything of it.

A proper mother would have, of course. Or probably anyone who had the first clue what they were doing.

Candy sank onto Dan's sofa and dropped her head in her hands. She was so tired. Not just from the immediate panic caused by Faith's illness and the blizzard, but from all the effort she'd been expending in recent weeks. Why on earth had she come here? Every time things started looking up, they somehow ended up going from bad to worse.

"You did the right thing," Dan said, moving to sit beside her. The warmth of his thigh pressing against hers was so comforting, she could have wept.

She gazed at him in the darkness. He was close enough to make out his features, and the reassuring smile on his face was a glimmer of light in the midst of such a strange, surreal night. "I did?"

"Yes, she should start feeling better soon. I've got some antibiotics in my medical bag I can give her, but I wanted to check with you first to make sure she doesn't have any allergies to medication I should know about."

Candy shook her head. "No, she doesn't."

At least Candy knew that much. She reached to run a soothing hand over Faith's head. At least the crying had stopped. Faith still fussed a bit, in between long, slow blinks.

"Good." Dan nodded. "Let me go give her some before she falls back asleep."

Candy felt herself smile—something she wouldn't have been able to imagine an hour ago. "Thank you. I mean it. I don't know what I would've done without this reverse house call."

He flashed her a wink. "I'm happy to help, but you would've figured things out. All parents go through this sort of thing, Candy. It's scary, particularly if you're on your own." He glanced around at their darkened surroundings. Outside, the wind howled. "And these are definitely some challenging circumstances, but you're a good mom. I don't want you to lose sight of that."

Candy's throat grew thick. He was saying all the right things, but why couldn't she seem to believe them?

"You're going to change your tune when you

realize I froze your pipes. I don't even know if I have enough bottled water for formula and baby cereal. I—"

"The two sides of the house have separate hot water heaters, separate pipes. When the cottage was made into a duplex some genius decided the plumbing on this New England home should go on the exterior walls. That's why your place has a pipe freezing problem and mine doesn't." His smile went lopsided, so boyishly charming that Candy almost forgot they were in the middle of a weather emergency. "It's okay, though. I'll share."

"Oh. Well…" She swallowed hard. "Okay, then."

"I'll finish getting Faith all settled and then we can build a fire and try and get the chill out of the air. In the meantime, there's a trunk full of blankets by the hearth. Feel free to wrap yourself up in one." He chuckled. "Or three."

Then he stood to carry Faith to the kitchen. Out of the corner of her eye, Candy spied a flash of velvety gray—Fancy, of course. She followed right on Dan's heels, tail held high.

"You pretend to hate him, but you don't, do you, cat?" Candy whispered.

Fancy paused to meow at her and then raced after the object of her not-so-secret crush.

She'd never related so much to a cat in her life.

Candy sighed. *You're not falling for him. You're just falling under the spell of his pediatric medical expertise and his free-flowing water. He's a literal port in a storm.*

That might be true right now, but the feelings stirring deep inside her weren't new. They'd been developing for days…weeks—since that very first awkward encounter she'd had with Dan at the gazebo. Sometimes it even felt like longer.

That was impossible, obviously. Again, Candy was probably just feeling overly emotional right now because her idyllic Vermont Christmas was ending so spectacularly. Technically, it was already Christmas Eve, wasn't it?

Candy hauled herself off the sofa. She couldn't think about that right now. Her ingredients for her snowman pancakes were sure to freeze over the next twenty-four hours if the power didn't come back on. She just wanted to close her eyes and hide under a pile of Dan's blankets until Christmas was over and done with.

* * *

Candy woke up later to the sound of a crackling fire and the sensation of warmth on her face. Blessed warmth!

She forgot where she was as she shook off sleep and let her eyes drift open. For a second, she felt like a kid again, waking up on Christmas morning, eager to run downstairs and see what Santa had left under the tree. Ready to run to her parents' bedroom and take a flying leap onto their bed until they stood, bleary-eyed, and followed her to the living room, where they'd sip coffee and watch her open her gifts.

But then the fire came into focus, blazing bright, and Candy noticed the sad little stocking hanging from the mantel. Her gaze shifted to the hearth, where Fancy sat calmly licking a paw and looking exactly as if she had zero intention of leaving Dan's house after the holidays were over. If ever.

She rubbed her eyes and glanced around the room. Her memory of what happened after Dan had given Faith her medicine was a bit fuzzy. Dan had gone next door and returned with Faith's bassinet in tow. Then he'd built a fire while Candy had rocked Faith until she'd fallen back asleep. After that, the rest was a sleepy, dreamy blur. She remembered helping Dan move all the furniture in the room closer to the fireplace so they could keep warm until the power came back on. Then she must have collapsed from sheer exhaustion.

Who knew how long she'd been asleep. And where was Dan, anyway?

She sat up, expecting to see him stretched out on the floor alongside Faith's bassinet. That's where she last remembered seeing him. They'd been talking as she'd drifted off to sleep. It had felt almost like a slumber party instead of what it really was—a snowed-in nightmare in the making.

He wasn't on the floor, though. Faith was still there, sleeping soundly in her familiar white cradle with her tiny chest rising and falling. In the glow from the fireplace, she looked like a Christmas cherub.

"Hello there, Sleeping Beauty," Dan said, echoing what he'd said to her the last time she'd slept on his sofa.

It wasn't the worst way to wake, Candy reluctantly admitted to herself. In fact, it was rather nice. She could have gotten quite used to it.

In another life, perhaps. Another time and place. Another Christmas.

"Why aren't you sleeping? It's still the middle of the night, isn't it?" She shifted under the cozy quilt she'd retrieved from Dan's antique trunk. Again, the same one she'd snuggled under the last time she'd spent the night with her not-quite-as-grumpy-as-she'd-thought neighbor.

Dan strolled into view, walking from the direction of the kitchen and carrying a bag of jumbo-sized marshmallows, a box of graham crackers and several chocolate candy bars.

"I couldn't sleep and the power is still out, so I thought I'd whip up a Christmas Eve treat that we could make in the fireplace."

Where to start?

Lovestruck's answer to Ebenezer Scrooge suddenly wanted to do something festive. And he just so happened to have the ingredients for her favorite campfire treat on hand?

She eyed his haul, focusing intently on the chocolate bars. They were the thick, jumbo size. No nuts. Her very favorite. "Am I dreaming, or are those the ingredients for s'mores?"

"You're not dreaming, although it's still the middle of the night. At least I think it is. With all the snow coming down, it's kind of hard to tell." He tossed the bag of marshmallows at her and she caught it just as Fancy tried to bat it away.

Maybe it was time to break the news to him that Fancy's stay was permanent. She had a feeling that no one had filled him in yet. She couldn't let the man rescue her during a blizzard and feed her Christmas s'mores without being completely honest with him.

"I hate to tell you this, but you have a cat now," Candy said.

Dan stopped in his tracks as his gaze slid toward Fancy, who'd retreated to her perch atop the Charlie Brown tree. "No. *No.* I'm just petsitting her until Ethel gets back from Florida."

Candy bit back a grin. Poor guy. "You mean the same Ethel who just moved into a new independent living apartment in Tampa?"

"You're kidding." Dan regarded her through narrowed eyes.

"Nope. I heard it from Frances, and as you know, she's a reliable source." Candy worked at opening the bag of marshmallows.

"Too reliable. Sometimes she seems to know what's going on in my life before I do."

"In this case, she definitely does," Candy said, and as if on cue, Fancy let out a booming meow. "I figured I should just rip off the

Band-Aid and tell you so you can get used to the idea."

Or make plans to take Fancy to a shelter, which Candy knew he would never consider. Not for a second.

Dan shook his head. "I've got a cat."

Of course he was going to keep Fancy. Only Dan Manning would let himself get tricked into adopting the town's most menacing feline.

"Told you," she said quietly. "You're a good guy. Who else would be able to produce s'mores out of nowhere like this?"

Candy's special Christmas morning pancakes ingredients were probably freezing in her dark refrigerator right now—yet another family tradition down the drain.

She tucked her legs underneath her and made room for Dan to sit down beside her. The pancakes didn't matter right now. Nothing did. It felt like the three of them were closed off from the rest of the world, and despite the circumstances, it was kind of…nice.

"I went on a first responder camping trip with the guys at the LFD last summer, and I was on s'mores duty." Dan dislodged the cardboard tube from a coat hanger and started fashioning it into a skewer for a marshmallow. "We never got around to making them."

"Seriously?" Candy grabbed the other coat hanger and got to work. "What else is there to do on a camping trip?"

"If you're a Lovestruck firefighter? Drink maple-flavored beer and spend all night trying to coerce the local pediatrician into signing up for a dating app." Dan speared a marshmallow onto a skewer and handed it to Candy.

She positioned it over the flame while she tried—and failed—not to ask him about his dating life. Hey, he'd been the one to bring it up. Didn't that make it fair game?

"So did you?" Why did she feel so nervous all of a sudden? "Sign up for an app, I mean?"

He kept his gaze aimed at the fire, where their marshmallows roasted, side by side. "No."

The relief that washed over her was ridiculous. She was leaving in less than twenty-four hours. Or she was supposed to, anyway. What did she care whom he dated?

"Why not?"

He shrugged one muscular, kitten-saving shoulder. "I don't date much. It's complicated."

Candy nodded as their marshmallows went

from white to toasty brown. "Kind of like your feelings about Christmas?"

Yep, she went there. She just couldn't help it.

This time was different, though. She wasn't going to tease him or try and pressure him into telling her why he felt the way he did about the holidays. She understood now. She got it.

For once, Dan didn't flinch or shy away from the discussion. He met her gaze full on as he sandwiched the marshmallow on her skewer between two graham cracker squares and a generous chunk of chocolate bar. "I guess you could say so, yes."

"I can't say that I blame you," Candy said.

He narrowed his gaze at her as she bit into her s'more and tried not to moan out loud. It was the best thing she'd ever tasted—even better than Christmas morning snowman pancakes.

Dan just sat staring at her, his s'more untouched. "Excuse me, but what happened to the Candy Cane I know and love? Did you just make a thinly veiled disparaging comment about Christmas spirit?"

The Candy Cane I know and love.

It was just an expression. Candy knew this, but her heart did a flip-flop, all the same.

She took another sloppy bite of s'more and hoped he'd chalk up the flush she felt creeping into her cheeks to the warmth of the fire. "I've decided you're right. I'm giving up on the Christmas thing. I did my best to make this year special for Faith, and it turned into an epic failure."

"What on earth are you talking about?" Dan looked at her with genuine shock written all over his features, as if he hadn't bore witness to her skating accident, her burned cookies, lackluster craft skills and host of other holiday disasters.

"This." She threw up her hands. "All of it. I tried. I really did, and if it hadn't been for you, Faith would be spending Christmas Eve with an ear infection and no water for baby formula while we froze to death upon a midnight clear."

He glanced at Faith, snug in her bassinet, and the lick of flames in the fireplace and then back at Candy. "I'm no expert, but as Christmases go, this one doesn't seem so bad."

Warmth spread through Candy's chest from the inside out. He was right.

Don't. You can't fall for him. Not while you've got one foot out the door.

"You realize I never got Faith's picture taken

with Santa, right?" she blurted. He was a pediatrician. Surely he'd know what a horrendous
breach of parental holiday etiquette that was,
even given his Grinchy streak.

Although, at the moment, she was the one
who sounded green and furry. Dan seemed fine.

Dare she think it? Borderline *festive*.

"So things didn't go exactly as you planned.
So what?" He shrugged again. Ugh, why
couldn't she stop staring at his shoulders? And
his chiseled jaw. And his lovely, lovely eyes. "I
think it's great what you've done for Faith this
Christmas. You love her. That's all that mat-
ters."

"Thank you for saying that." Her throat
closed. "I just can't do it in real life, though.
I thought I could, but I can't. There's just so
much pressure surrounding the holidays. Make-
believe I can handle. The real thing?" She let
out a shaky laugh. "Not so much, apparently."

He gave her a look so probing that she nearly
forgot how to breathe. "Sometimes the best
Christmas moments are unscripted, though,
don't you think?"

Moments like the gazebo.

And moments like this one—right here, right
now. With him.

Candy swallowed. *My gosh, he's right.*

"Seriously, Candy." The smile that came to his lips was so sad that the lump in her throat tripled in size. "Don't be like me. You're perfect just the way you are."

She didn't dare say a word. She wanted so badly to know what had happened to make him feel the way he did about Christmas, but she wasn't going to press. Not again.

Still, the question hung in the empty space between them like a snowflake, fleeting and impossible to catch hold of. Unasked. Unanswered.

Until Dan met her gaze and, at long last, told Candy the truth.

Chapter Fifteen

"There was a fire."

The words were out of Dan's mouth before he could stop them.

He hadn't intended on telling Candy what happened. He would have been perfectly happy letting her leave without knowing a thing about his past. He'd come so close, too…

But then she'd started talking like someone who didn't believe in Christmas magic—someone like him. And he just couldn't take it, couldn't fathom Candy without her silly holiday sweaters and a tree in every room. Dan didn't want her to lose that part of herself. Her love for Christmas and the hope she carried in her heart were some of the things that made Candy who she was—things Dan wanted to help her protect at all costs. Not just for her sake, but for Faith's, too.

For *his*. Couldn't she see how much knowing her these past few weeks had changed him?

Maybe not, because he'd been doing his level best to keep her at arm's length, clinging to the absurd notion that letting her in—letting *anyone* in—would open himself up to more pain. More hurt. Maybe he'd spent so many Decembers trying to hold himself together that he was incapable of showing her how he felt. If that was true, then he'd simply have to tell her.

"My parents were having their annual Christmas Eve party. It was always a big neighborhood affair and my mom had been in the kitchen cooking all day." Dan paused to take a deep inhale as he let himself revisit the memory of those happy Christmases. "She used to make an entire gingerbread village every year, with spun sugar windows and coconut snow."

Candy gave him a tender smile, but kept quiet, giving him the time and space he needed to piece together the memories. Dan had never told anyone about the events of his seventh Christmas. Ever. It was hard to know where to start.

He closed his eyes, but all he saw was smoke—thick, black smoke. And then his little brother's face, covered with bandages as he lay still in a hospital bed.

"I wanted to help, so while my parents were getting dressed and ready for the party, I decided to light the candles on the Advent wreath I'd made in Sunday school. It sat on the center of the dining room table, surrounded by cakes and cookies, like it was my mom's pride and joy, even though it was just a kid's holiday craft project." He glanced from the crackling logs in the fireplace to Candy, and the look in her eyes told him that he didn't need to say any more. She knew where this story was going.

But he needed to finish, needed to get it all out in the open. Maybe if he did, he wouldn't feel like he was still choking on that smoke, even all these years later.

"I couldn't reach the center of the table, so I stood on a chair. My little brother held it still for me, but I had to lean over so far that I lost my balance and dropped the match." He shook his head. It was strange how something that happened in just a split second could change everything. Dan still had a hard time wrapping his mind around it. "My brother and I were so shocked by the flames that we didn't move at first. We just stood there, staring at the fire like it was imaginary."

Candy reached for his hand, squeezed it hard and finally spoke. "Oh, Dan. You were just a kid."

"A kid who burned down his family home and put his kid brother in the hospital," he said quietly. "It didn't take long for flames to race around the table. There was an old decorative oil lamp and other combustibles that turned my childish mistake into a conflagration."

Shame coursed through him, but when he let himself look Candy in the eye, he didn't see blame or horror there. Just the same unspeakable sadness that had been his companion for over half of his life.

"My parents were fine. I was fine. But Scotty had burns to his face and left arm. He spent a month in the hospital and had several skin graft surgeries. We're still close, actually. I was the best man at his wedding last year, but my family knows to give me space this time of year. I just—" he shook his head "—can't. For years afterward, my mom and dad did their best to make a big deal out of Christmas. They still wanted it to be a special time for us. They tried everything—vacations, trips. You name it. When I got to be an adult, I simply told them I'd rather spend the holidays on my own."

Candy nodded, eyes filling with tears. "I understand. And I'm sorry I pushed. So, so sorry."

"Don't apologize." He shook his head. "Please. It's not your fault..."

"It's not yours either, though. Not anymore. You made a mistake when you were a child. It doesn't have to define you for the rest of your life."

But it did. Every single day.

"You're a pediatrician because of your brother, aren't you?" Candy said. "And this is also why you do so much volunteer work with the fire department."

Dan nodded, not quite trusting himself to speak.

"So maybe it does define you, but in a good way. This terrible thing has turned you into the man you are today. A *good* man." She squeezed his hand so hard that he thought it might break.

And something inside him broke along with it. She still thought of him as good, but more than that... She made him *feel* that way. Candy made him feel like a kind and decent person, even when he'd been so foolishly intent on trying to prove himself otherwise.

He reached to cup her face in his hands. If she took one thing away from this conversation, he wanted it to be this. "What I'm trying to say is please don't change. Please don't stop believing in Christmas. Because when you do, sometimes that hope becomes lost forever."

Sometimes, but Dan was beginning to think maybe not always. Maybe not even now...

Tell her the rest.

His thoughts screamed and his heart felt like it might beat right out of his chest. She still only knew part of the story—the very worst of it. There was an important piece to the puzzle still buried deep, glowing like an ember...the tiniest possible spark of hope that he'd carried with him for years. And the glow of it was slowly becoming enough to overcome his darkness.

"Candy..." He ran his fingertips gently over her red ribbon lips. "My sweet, sweet Candy."

And before he could say another word, she pressed her mouth to his and kissed him as if she could breathe new life into his soul. She tasted of chocolate and marshmallows. Of innocence. Of the childhood holidays he was slowly coming to associate with something other than guilt and sorrow and pain.

Then there was no more talking, no more remembering. Everything was warm and wonderful and new as a bitter-cold Christmas Eve gave way to a radiant and glittering Christmas morning.

They kissed for hours.

Candy lost all track of time as day and night blurred into a marshmallow-sweet dream of tender whispers, tending to Faith together and sleeping in the soft glow of the fire. Miraculously, she forgot all about the storm until she woke up in Dan's arms on Christmas morning to sunlight streaming through the windows.

"I think it finally stopped snowing," she murmured into the crook of Dan's neck.

He dragged his eyes open and looked at her in the gold morning light. "So it has. A Christmas miracle."

"A Christmas miracle," she echoed, throat clogging now that she knew how hard it was for him to say those particular words. "This may sound silly since Faith is only a baby, but I want to see if I can sneak next door, get her presents and arrange them under your tree before she wakes up."

Dan's face cracked into a sleepy smile. "It doesn't sound silly at all. It sounds sweet." He sat up and scrubbed a hand over his face. "Let me go out and brave the cold, though. I might have to dig my way to your place."

He hopped up and pulled one of his soft cashmere sweaters over his head, along with a coat and boots that looked heavy and warm enough to trek all the way to the North Pole. Then, with a wink, he grabbed a snow shovel from the mudroom and headed out the front door.

Faith's fever had broken during the night, and when she began babbling happily in her bassinet, Candy could have cried from sheer relief. It wasn't until she'd given the baby a fresh diaper and changed her into clean footie pajamas—decorated with little candy canes, of course—that she realized she wasn't shivering while she moved about Dan's house. Red numbers flashed on the clock on the microwave.

The power was back!

By the time Dan returned, juggling the gifts that had been piled under Candy's tree, Faith had finished her breakfast and the house smelled like freshly brewed coffee and peppermint cream.

Fancy batted balls of crumpled wrapping paper around the house as they helped Faith open her gifts. It wasn't long until she grew sleepy again, so Candy moved her bassinet to Dan's bedroom and tucked her in with one of her new toys—a soft, floppy bunny that she'd bought at Melanie's store. When she returned to the living room, Dan was standing beside the Charlie Brown tree with a small wrapped box in his hand.

"It looks like we forgot one," he said, holding up the gift.

"Actually, that one isn't for Faith." Candy shrugged. "It's for you."

His mouth curved into a boyish grin. "You got me a Christmas present?"

"I sure did."

"Well, isn't that a coincidence. I got one for you, too." He held up a finger. "Wait here."

Candy wrapped her arms around herself, unable to stop smiling while she waited. He came back seconds later, carrying a flat package.

"You go first," she said, nodding toward his gift. "It's just a little something I saw at one of the boutiques on Main Street and had to buy because it's got your name written all over it."

Dan unwrapped the box, crunched the paper into a ball and tossed it at Fancy, who attacked it with gusto. Then he lifted the lid, pulled a ceramic mug from inside and let out a bark of laughter.

"Cat Dad?" He turned the mug to show off the letters splashed across its front. "Nice. I guess I'm truly stuck with that monster now."

Candy rolled her eyes. "Oh, please. She had you at meow and you know it. The *entire town* knows it."

"Guilty." He flashed her a wink and pulled her in for a long, lingering kiss. "Thank you. I love it. Now you go."

He nodded toward the flat package—the only remaining wrapped gift under the tree.

Candy picked it up, nervous all of a sudden. She couldn't remember the last time someone had given her a present on Christmas morning. Gabe was a good friend and a great boss, but not much of a gift giver. Candy liked to shower the crew with little trinkets during the holidays, but gifts had never played much of a role in her Christmases as an adult. Christmas mornings belonged to people with families.

Her hands shook a bit as she lifted the tape and peeled back the paper, revealing the corner of a carved wooden frame. And then she caught a glimpse of the photograph inside the frame and her fingertips flew to her mouth.

"Oh my gosh." Tears filled her eyes until the image before her looked like a watercolor painting, and still she couldn't tear her gaze away from it. "It's Faith. And Santa."

The picture showed a beaming Faith, sitting on Santa's lap in the classic pose, just the way Candy had always imagined it in her head. It was the Christmas keepsake she'd had her heart set on all along, but thought she'd never have.

"I don't understand." She shook her head. "How did you—"

Her words stuttered to a halt as she got a closer look at Santa's face. She knew the lopsided smile hiding beneath the elaborate white beard, just as she knew those soulful blue eyes that never failed to make her weak in the knees.

She gasped. "It's you."

Dan Manning—the same man who'd wanted to permanently deflate her reindeer lawn ornament, who'd only acquiesced to getting the world's most pathetic Christmas tree under duress and whose feelings about the holidays were filled with nothing but sadness and regret—had somehow procured a Santa suit and posed for a picture with Faith, just so Candy could have the one Christmas gift she most wanted.

"I can't believe you did this." She shook her head, unable to form the words to tell him how much the photograph meant to her.

"Frances told me how upset you were about missing the chance for a Santa photo when the Christmas festival shut down early. When Felicity babysat Faith the other day so you could pack, I sort of borrowed your baby. I hope you don't mind," he said.

Candy laughed. "Not at all. This is the most special thing anyone has ever done for me... aside from rescuing me during a snowstorm."

"We rescued each other, sweetheart." He brushed a tear from her cheek with a gentle swipe of his thumb. "I might have to stop telling Frances to mind her own business, after all."

"This is perfect." Candy held the picture to her heart. "I don't even know how to thank you."

He pulled her close and held her while she cried. She didn't know what had come over her all of a sudden. The gift was special, so special, but why was she suddenly falling to pieces?

You know why, a little voice in the back of her head said.

The storm had ended. Her bags were packed and ready to go. Once the roads were clear, she'd be on her way to Burlington to catch her flight.

Christmas was over.

Don't panic. It hasn't ended yet. There's still time to figure things out. She couldn't leave— not now. Not when everything between the two of them had changed.

She couldn't... And she wouldn't. The blizzard had barely ended. There was no way her flight was going to leave on time. She would have bet money on it. Gabe would understand if she got back to LA a day or two late, wouldn't he? He'd have to, given that Candy didn't have any control over the situation.

A tremble started deep in her bones.

And then what? What happens once the snow clears? You're just going to walk away and never look back? She needed to do something—say something, *any*thing—to stop the rest of this day from unfolding.

"Dan," she whispered into his shoulder.

But it was too little, too late. Her still, small voice was drowned out by the sound of a knock on Dan's door.

Chapter Sixteen

"Wade." Dan shifted from one foot to the other and tried to figure out why his friend had turned up at his door unannounced on Christmas morning. At the tail end of a winter storm, no less. "Hey."

"Merry Christmas." Wade held up a hand. Behind him, the yard sparkled under a blanket of pristine, new-fallen snow. Down the street, a snowplow was already making its way through the historic district, paving the way for life to return to normal. They'd been running all night, not waiting for an insurmountable pile of snow to collect on roads.

The thought struck Dan as profoundly sad. For once, he wasn't quite ready for the holidays to be over.

"Merry Christmas," he said. The words came a bit easier now than they used to. "Come in. It's freezing out there."

He held the door open wide, but Wade didn't move. He just stood there, jammed his hands in his pockets and glanced toward Candy's door. "Actually, I was looking for Candy. I rang the bell, but she's not answering. You don't happen to know where she is, do you?"

Dan nodded. "She's here with me."

"I thought she might be here," Wade said, but there wasn't a trace of humor in his tone.

Odd. Wade didn't ordinarily hold back when he had thoughts about Dan's personal life. There was zero chance that Felicity hadn't told him about Dan taking the Santa photos with Faith as a Christmas gift for Candy. He was sure to have opinions. Some good-natured teasing about his love life would have been the norm in this scenario, but the look on Wade's face as he strode inside the house was carefully neutral as Candy approached the door.

"Wade, hi." Candy smiled at him and moved in for a hug and another round of Merry Christmases. If she'd been expecting Wade to come looking for her, she didn't give any indication whatsoever.

While the three of them chatted about the storm, Dan noticed Wade sneaking glances at the two of them, brow furrowing.

"So, I'm sorry to just come out and ask, because it feels like I've interrupted something here." Wade sighed. "But, um, do you still need a ride to the airport, Candy?"

Dan's gut hardened.

So, this was it?

"That's why you're here?" Candy went pale.

Wade nodded. "Yeah. I know Felicity volunteered to take you and Faith to Burlington for your flight, but some of the roads are still a mess. I've got the fire department's SUV out front. I should be able to get you there no problem. You didn't get any of Felicity's messages? She called earlier to let you know I'd be here a couple hours before you two had planned to head out, just in case we run into more bad weather."

"My phone ran out of charge when the power

was out. I haven't even checked to see if my flight has been canceled," Candy said.

"It hasn't. The airport is up and running. This is Vermont, remember? We're not going to let one small blizzard shut us down. We'll get you out of here, right on schedule." Now that the mystery of Wade's sudden appearance had been cleared up, he sounded downright cheery.

Dan, on the other hand, could feel himself slipping back into Grinch mode—more and more with each passing second.

"Oh." Candy's gaze fixed with Dan's and then she quickly looked away. "That's great?"

It sounded more like a question than a statement. Was Dan supposed to weigh in? Because he didn't think leaving for the airport sounded great at all.

But Candy couldn't seem to meet his gaze anymore. She'd started piling Faith's gifts into a neat stack. The photo he'd given her was soon lost beneath a pile of stuffed animals and baby onesies.

Dan knew not to read anything into what was happening. Candy had plans. Her stay in Lovestruck was never supposed to be permanent. She was going to go back to a place where Christmas came every day while Dan put another blue December behind him and welcomed the fresh start of a new month. A new year. A new beginning.

It was Dan's favorite annual ritual. He looked forward to it each and every one of the thirty-one days of December. Now...

Well now, the thought of January left him with a knot in the pit of his stomach.

It's only a day, he reminded himself. Christmas was fleeting, no matter how hard anyone tried to hold on to it, and Candy was practically Christmas herself.

"I'm going to go next door to change. I'll be right back," she said. "If you could look after Faith for a few minutes?"

Dan nodded. "Of course. Take your time."

Take all the time in the world.

She left, and the sunshine seemed to follow her. Even Fancy seemed to notice. The cat let loose with a forlorn meow from her perch inside the top branches of the Christmas tree.

Wade's eyes went wide. His gaze flitted from place to place in the living room. "Why did that howl sound so familiar?"

Dan shrugged. "It's Fancy. You know I brought her here after she got stuck in Ethel's tree the other day. Ethel is in Florida."

He left out the part about Ethel's move being permanent. He simply didn't have it in him to engage in a conversation about the cat right now.

"Of course I remember. It just never occurred to me that you would let that beast *inside your house.*"

"What was I supposed to do? Leave her outside in a blizzard?"

"Given her personality?" Wade raised his eyebrows, pretending to weigh the merits of the nonpossibility, and then his gaze snagged on the mug Candy had given him for Christmas. *"Cat Dad?"*

He burst out laughing.

Dan glared at him. "Laugh it up. I'm going to go check on Faith."

Dan headed toward the bedroom, but, of course, Wade trotted behind him like a loyal, albeit annoying, dog.

"I'm a pediatrician, remember? I can handle the baby on my own."

"Clearly." Wade shot a wary glance over his shoulder. "But you're not leaving me alone in here with that monster."

"She's not that bad," Dan heard himself say, despite the late-night kitchen raids, the stealth attacks on his ankles when he dared to walk across a room and Fancy's various off-key vocalizations. "She's misunderstood."

Faith peered up from inside her bassinet and when her big blue eyes landed on Dan, her sweet little mouth curved into a giggly smile. Dan's chest felt like it was on the verge of caving in.

How was he going to do this? How was he going to say goodbye? Not just to Candy, but to Faith, too?

"Come here, little one," he murmured, gathering Faith into his arms. She snuggled her soft head against him until they were cheek to cheek.

Wade's gaze narrowed. "What are you doing?"

"I'm holding a baby. You have a son at home, remember? This should look really familiar," Dan joked.

But Wade wasn't about to fall for distraction by way of sarcasm. "Don't. I'm trying to be real with you for a second."

Faith gathered a handful of Dan's sweater into her tiny fist. The gray cashmere may as well have been his heart.

"'Cat Dad?'" Wade arched an eyebrow.

"Playing house during the storm? And I don't ever remember seeing a Christmas tree in your living room or a stocking hanging from your mantel before. Granted, they're both a little pathetic looking. You might need to do some shopping at next year's Christmas festival."

Dan's jaw tensed. "Don't insult my stocking."

What was *wrong* with him? There was no denying that the stocking was objectively terrible. Fancy could have probably done a better job using just her claws and a ball of yarn.

But Dan loved that thing. It was perfect, just the way it was. Earnest and heartfelt, just like the woman who'd made it.

"So that's how it is." Wade nodded and crossed his arms, looking every inch like a firefighter readying himself to enter a burning building.

"What?" Dan said, even though he knew full well what was coming next.

"You have feelings for Candy."

He shook his head, because he couldn't seem to force the words *no, I don't* from his mouth.

"Don't lie to me." Wade jabbed a pointer finger in Dan's direction. "It's Christmas, and at Christmas you tell the truth. It's a rule."

"Did you just quote *Love Actually* to me?"

Wade's gaze narrowed again. "You've seen it?"

Fine. So maybe Dan had watched a few holiday movies in secret through the years. And maybe a few of them had been the sentimental, made-for-television movies that Candy loved so much. It wasn't a crime. Even the most hardened of Grinches caved and watched those from time to time, right?

"Aha! You're a romantic—a romantic who loves Christmas," Wade said in a tone that was both accusatory and joyful, all at the same time. "And you have feelings for a woman named Candy Cane."

Was it that obvious? Apparently so.

Wade wasn't finished with his observations, because of course he wasn't. Dan might seriously need to consider moving to a town where at least some of the citizens respected personal boundaries.

"Those are undeniable facts, my friend," Wade said. "Only one question remains—what are you going to do about it?"

The front door to Dan's house opened and closed. Candy was back, and ready to let Wade usher her right out of Dan's life.

What are you going to do about it?

If he'd been in a movie, Dan would have

had a boom box and stack of posters ready to deal with the situation. But real life was more complicated than a movie. More risky. More painful. And as much as Dan was tempted to spend his Christmas performing a dramatic, last-minute dash through an airport or some other festive grand gesture, he couldn't do it. He wouldn't have even known where to begin.

He was on the road to healing, thanks to Candy. But he couldn't completely change overnight. Old habits died hard. Once Candy was gone, Christmas could go back to being just a day on the calendar for him. That kind of life had served Dan well for over twenty years. He knew how to live that way. He was good at it. Maybe at times it made him miserable, like Fancy getting herself stuck at the top of a tree, but at least he was safe and so was his heart.

What was the alternative?

Were he and Candy supposed to turn their lives upside down for a brief holiday fling?

It's more than that, and you know it.

Dan knew it, but Candy didn't.

If this was fate…if Christmas magic was a real thing and it had wrapped itself around them and chosen Dan and Candy for lifelong love, wouldn't she know? Wouldn't she remember?

He *needed* her to remember. Candy was love and optimism and hope. Dan was none of those things. He needed her to believe for the both of them.

"What am I going to do about it?" he finally said under his breath. "Nothing, okay? Candy and I are going to say goodbye and you're going to take her to the airport as planned."

Merry freaking Christmas.

The goodbyes were awkward, made even more so by Wade's presence. Candy was almost glad for that, though, because with him there, at least she could maintain her composure.

Mostly.

Tears pricked her eyes as Dan buckled Faith into her car seat in the back of the LFD utility vehicle. He and Wade packed all of her luggage into the back of the SUV with startling efficiency as the minutes seemed to tick past with alarming speed.

All the while, the beauty of Lovestruck completely covered in glittering white was so gorgeous that it was painful to look at. Candy couldn't help thinking about all the sets she'd worked on where they'd used foam snow or snow made from recycled paper and blown into the scene for a "natural" effect. What a joke. She'd never realized how far off from the real thing it looked. Maybe all those perfect, artificial Christmases she'd created over the years hadn't been quite as perfect as she'd thought.

Because none of them were real. Her throat grew tight as Wade slid into the driver's seat and Dan held the car door open for her. *But this one was.*

"Thank you," she said, holding her Vuitton tote tight to her chest. She'd tucked the picture of Dan dressed as Santa with Faith in his lap deep inside its leathery confines, because she couldn't bear the thought of losing it if the airline lost track of her luggage. "For everything, I mean. This was one of the nicest Christmases I've ever had."

"Mine, too," he said, but the wonder she'd seen in his eyes a few hours ago was gone. All she saw there now was sadness.

She took a deep breath and gave him a final once-over, wanting to capture everything about him in her memory. But then she changed her mind.

This wasn't the Dan she wanted to remember. Candy wanted to remember the Dan who'd chopped down trees for her and made her s'mores. The Dan who dressed up as Santa, took care of her when she had a sprained ankle and drank out of a mug that said Cat Dad. *That* Dan wouldn't have let her walk away like this.

That Dan would have asked her to stay, at least until New Year's Eve.

Would she, though? Would she've stayed?

Candy had all but begged Gabe to take her back. Being fired had felt like losing the biggest and most important part of herself. She didn't know who she was without her job.

Then, strangely enough, she'd found herself in the most unlikely of places. She'd come to Lovestruck because she wanted to give the gift of Christmas to Faith, but Candy's life had been changed, too. She felt at home here, despite all of her various missteps. The next time she got snowed in, she would definitely know to drip her faucets and keep her phone fully charged.

But there wouldn't be a next time, would there?

"Goodbye, Dan." The tremor in her voice was almost her undoing.

Ask me. She locked eyes with him. *Ask me to stay.*

"Goodbye, Candy Cane," he said, and then

he turned around and went back inside the house before she'd even climbed inside the car.

Okay, then. It was time to act like a big girl and make polite conversation with Wade all the way to Burlington. She could cry her eyes out once she was on the plane.

She got inside the SUV, clicked her seat belt in place and slammed the door hard enough to cause an avalanche.

Candy kept her gaze glued forward as Wade maneuvered the vehicle slowly through Lovestruck's charming historic district. Snow was piled high along the picket fences and the decorative Victorian trim of the homes, as if they weren't in a real town at all, but had somehow left Lovestruck and ended up in one of Dan's mom's gingerbread villages. Snowmen waved their stick arms at her as they drove past. Smoke curled from the chimneys while families inside gathered around the Christmas tree to open gifts. Maybe some of them dined on special Christmas morning pancakes.

Or s'mores.

She turned toward Wade as they came to the stop sign where they'd veer right onto Main Street. "Thank you again for doing this. I know you'd much rather be home with Felicity and Nick."

"Are you kidding? Our kiddo has been up for hours already. I promise I don't mind," he said, and the look he gave her was filled with so much pity that Candy wanted to crawl into the glove box and hide.

He turned his gaze back toward the windshield, but made no move to put his foot on the accelerator, despite the fact that there wasn't a car in sight. Main Street was a beautiful blank slate of white.

"About Dan," he started, but the cell phone in the cup holder between them chimed with an incoming text, preventing him from saying more.

Saved by the proverbial bell, Candy thought. She didn't want to discuss Dan with Wade. It would be too heartbreaking, not to mention a possible violation of Dan's privacy. She just needed to get on the plane and get out of this picture-perfect town and not look back.

"Sorry," Wade said, reaching for the phone. "I've got to check this. I'm on standby for the department today. Cap always staffs the firehouse as sparsely as possible on the holidays so we can spend time with our families."

"Sure thing," Candy said. "I hope it's nothing dire."

Wade put the car in Park, tapped the phone's small screen and scrolled through a lengthy text with a flick of his thumb. A grin flashed on his face, but only for a split second. He quickly rearranged his features and returned the phone to the cup holder.

"Nothing dire, but I've got to stop by the firehouse and take care of something real quick before we head out of town. I hope you don't mind?" He shifted the SUV back into Drive.

"Oh." She sagged a little in her seat. Saying goodbye to Dan had nearly broken her, and now she had to do the same to Lovestruck. Making a clean, speedy getaway really would have helped. This long goodbye was torture, but LFD business obviously took priority. "Do what you need to do. Safety first."

Was it her imagination, or did Wade seem to drive almost comically slowly toward the firehouse? Main Street had obviously been plowed relatively recently, being the town's main thoroughfare and all. They were still the only vehicle on the road, but it took them several long minutes to crawl toward the station. And when they finally pulled into the apparatus bay, Wade seemed to just sit there as if trying to remember why they'd stopped by in the first place.

"I need to go take care of something," he said, giving a whole new meaning to the word *vague*.

"Yes, you mentioned that." Candy gave him a sideways glance.

Was there really some sort of nonurgent LFD emergency he needed to attend do? Candy was beginning to wonder.

"I'll be back in a few." He flashed her a smile so full of charm that Candy might have envied Felicity her darling family…

If only Candy hadn't left her heart back at the home of a certain cranky doctor and his even crankier cat.

She took a few deep, calming breaths and tried to talk herself into calming down, much the same way she'd done for temperamental actors a time or two.

This feeling is temporary. Once I leave town, everything will be fine.

But what if Candy didn't want to be fine anymore? What if she no longer wanted fake snow and gingerbread houses made of cardboard? Icicles made of plastic and Christmas kisses that took an entire team of people to orchestrate?

What if she wanted the real deal—unplanned, unscripted and perfectly imperfect?

She let the question swirl in her thoughts while Wade was away, until the idea took root way down deep in her soul. And then she finally allowed herself to say the impossible out loud.

"What if we didn't go back, Faith?"

Candy closed her eyes, heart pounding, and wished more than anything that Faith could tell her what to do. She wasn't used to making decisions for two people. She'd been on her own for so, so long. Faith meant the world to her, and she wanted to make the right choices— good and meaningful choices—for them both.

But, of course, Faith couldn't give her the answers. She was just a baby. Candy had to figure things out on her own, and if she stayed in Lovestruck, what would she possibly do for work? It wasn't as if rural Vermont had a high demand for assistant film directors.

I need a sign. A true Christmas miracle.

She glanced heavenward, but all she could see was the ceiling of the SUV, outfitted with spaces for firefighting gear. Candy wasn't surprised. She had a feeling she'd used up more than her fair share of Christmas magic while snowed in with Dan.

"Ready?" Wade asked as he yanked open the driver's side door and slid back inside the car.

Candy nodded, but with a pang of uncertainty in the place where her heart should be.

"Everything okay in there?" she asked, nodding toward the firehouse.

Wade checked his phone one last time and then tucked it into the pocket of his LFD jacket. "Yep. Everything is A-OK."

He smiled at her and put the car into Reverse. Within seconds, they were back on Main Street, cruising past Melanie's store, Alice's yarn shop, the Bean and all the other places that Candy had fallen in love with while she'd been in Lovestruck. They no longer seemed to be crawling at a snail's pace. In fact, it felt like the car was flying, swallowing up the space between her and Dan.

Candy gripped the armrest as the towering town Christmas tree came into view. Just beyond the boughs of the great evergreen stood the gazebo. She wasn't ready to leave that special place behind. It still represented everything she loved about Lovestruck, about Christmas. For years, she'd been chasing a memory of that perfect Christmas kiss and against all odds, she'd found it.

Same town, different man. Who would've thought?

Except there'd been something awfully familiar about the look in Dan's eyes when he'd taken her face in his hands and kissed her by the fire while snow spun in the midnight blue sky. Something that had made Candy's heart crack open wide. She'd been so overwhelmed by the feel of his mouth against hers, the sublime warmth of him and the knowledge that he'd opened his heart to her, even though it hurt. Even if it wasn't for forever...

And in the sheer perfection of the moment, she hadn't even realized that her two snowy Christmas Eve kisses had been one and the same.

"Turn around," she whispered. Her pulse was booming so fast that she could barely form words.

"What?" Wade swiveled his head to glance at her.

"I said turn around," she said, louder this time. Loud enough to rouse Faith, who let loose with a stream of baby talk in the back seat. "I need to go back."

She implored Wade with her gaze, so intent on getting him to turn the car around that she was barely aware that they'd stopped moving. He'd pulled the SUV to the curb just beyond the big tree. It rose up behind him, as if welcoming visitors to Lovestruck with its sweeping, snow-laden arms.

"Candy," he said with a tender smile. Then he cast a glance over her shoulder. "Turn around, sweetheart."

With her heart in her throat, she did as he said. The gazebo sat directly behind her, strewn in Christmas lights, a glittering star on the snowy horizon. But the gazebo itself wasn't the sight that made her gasp—it was the giant, twelve-foot inflatable reindeer that stood in front of it...

And the man waiting for on the bench where she'd first kissed him at the tender age of sixteen.

Candy fumbled with the door handle, desperate to get out of the car. Her hands shook so fiercely that Wade had to lean over and unfasten her seat belt for her. And then she was stumbling through the snow, lungs burning from the crisp winter air as she ran toward her future.

Toward Dan.

He rose up from the bench and met her halfway, beneath Rudolph's enormous bobbing head. And when he caught her in his arms, she grabbed onto him like she'd never let go.

"It was you," she said through a fresh wave of tears. "All those years ago, it was you, wasn't it?"

Dan kissed the damp tears from her face and whispered against her ear, "It's always been you and me, Candy."

She didn't know whether to cry or laugh. It felt like she was experiencing every possible emotion, all at the same time. But when one of Rudolph's massive antlers bonked Dan on the head, she settled on laughter. And joy. It was Christmas, after all.

"So this is what Wade's stalling tactics were all about." She shook her head, grinning from ear to ear. As it turned out, life's unscripted moments could be even more perfect than the ones that had been crafted to leave audiences breathless. "I can't believe you dragged my reindeer down here."

"It seemed like the most obvious way to get your attention so I could tell you how sorry I am for letting you walk away when all I've wanted to do since the sun came up was ask you to stay."

"It's a sign," Candy said.

"It's a grand gesture," Dan corrected, eyes dancing. "Like from one of your movies."

Then she rose up on tiptoe and lifted her face to his, and in the moment just before their lips met, she murmured against his warm, familiar mouth, "This isn't at all like the movies."

His blue eyes found hers, and in their soulful depths, she saw it all—their Christmas Past, the Christmas Present and the Christmas Future they'd build together as a family, right here in Lovestruck.

"It's better."

* * * * *

WE HOPE YOU ENJOYED
THIS BOOK FROM

⊞HARLEQUIN
SPECIAL
EDITION

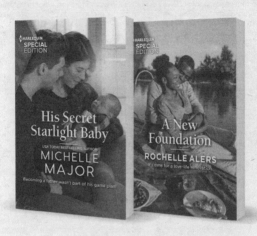

Believe in love. Overcome obstacles. Find happiness.

Relate to finding comfort and strength in the
support of loved ones and enjoy the journey
no matter what life throws your way.

6 NEW BOOKS AVAILABLE EVERY MONTH!

#2881 THEIR NEW YEAR'S BEGINNING
The Fortunes of Texas: The Wedding Gift • by Michelle Major

Brian Fortune doesn't think he will ever find the woman he kissed at his brother's New Year's wedding. So when the search for the provenance of a mysterious gift leads him into a local antique store a few days later, he's stunned to find Emmaline Lewis, proprietor—and mystery kisser! Brian has never been the type to commit, but suddenly he knows he'll do anything to stay at Emmaline's side—for good.

#2882 HER HOMETOWN MAN
Sutton's Place • by Shannon Stacey

Summoned home by her mother and sisters, novelist Gwen Sutton has made it clear—she's not staying. She's returning to her quiet life as soon as the family brewery is up and running. But when Case Danforth offers his help, it's clear there's more than just beer brewing! Time is short for Case to convince Gwen that a home with him is where her heart is.

#2883 THE RANCHER'S BABY SURPRISE
Texas Cowboys & K-9s • by Sasha Summers

Former soldier John Mitchell has come home after being discharged and asks to stay with his best friend, Natalie. They're both in for a shock when a precious baby girl is left on Natalie's doorstep—and John is the father! Now John needs Natalie's help more than ever. But Natalie has been in love with John forever. How can she help him find his way to being a family man if she's not part of that family?

#2884 THE CHARMING CHECKLIST
Charming, Texas • by Heatherly Bell

Max Del Toro persuaded his friend Ava Long to play matchmaker in exchange for posing as her boyfriend for one night. He even gave her a list of must-haves for his future wife. Except now he can't stop thinking about Ava—who doesn't check a single item on his list!

#2885 HIS LOST AND FOUND FAMILY
Sierra's Web • by Tara Taylor Quinn

Learning he's guardian to his orphaned niece sends architect Michael O'Connell's life into a tailspin. He's floored by the responsibility, so when Mariah Anderson agrees to pitch in at home, Michael thinks she's heaven-sent. He's shocked at the depth of his own connection to Mariah and opens his heart to her in ways he never imagined. But can an instant family turn into a forever one?

#2886 A CHEF'S KISS
Small Town Secrets • by Nina Crespo

Small-town chef Philippa Gayle's onetime rival-turned-lover Dominic Crawford upended her life. But when she's forced together with the celebrity cook on a project that could change her life, there's no denying that the flames that were lit years ago were only banked, not extinguished. Can Philippa trust Dominic enough to let him in...or are they just cooking up another heartbreak?

HSECNM1221

"I'd like to take you out on a proper date then."

"Okay." Color bloomed in her cheeks. "That would be
nice." He leaned in, but she held up a finger. "You should
know that since Kirby and the gang outed my pregnancy
at the coffee shop, I'm not going to hide it anymore." She
pressed a hand to her belly. "I'm wearing a baggy shirt
tonight because it seemed easier than fielding questions
from the boys, but if we go out, there will be questions.
And comments."

"I don't care about what anyone else thinks," he
assured her and then kissed her gently. "This is about you
and me."

Those must have been the right words, because Emmaline wound her arms around his neck and drew closer. "I'm glad," she said, but before he could kiss her again, she yawned once more.

"I'll walk you to your car."

She mock pouted but didn't argue. "I'm definitely not as fun as I used to be," she told him as he picked up the bags with the leftover supplies to carry for her. "Actually I'm not sure I was ever that fun."

"As far as I'm concerned, you're the best."

After another lingering kiss, Emmaline climbed into her car and drove away. Brian watched her taillights until they disappeared around a bend. The night sky overhead was once again filled with stars, and he breathed in the fresh Texas air. He needed to stay in the moment and remember his reason for being in town and how long he planned to stay. He knew better than to examine the feeling of contentment coursing through him.

One thing he knew for certain was that it couldn't last.

Don't miss
Their New Year's Beginning *by Michelle Major,*
available January 2022 wherever
Harlequin Special Edition books and ebooks are sold.

Harlequin.com